A GENTLEMAN'S KISS

Once they reached the upper landing window, Robert's temper grew more tranquil. Furthermore, he did not set Isobel in one of the corner chairs, as she had expected, but continued to hold her in his arms. "I like this view," he said.

"Yes," she agreed. "It is beautiful."

While they enjoyed the bucolic scene in companionable silence, Robert rested his chin against the top of her head. Isobel was certain he must be lost in thought and unaware of what he did, for moments later she felt his lips brush her temple. "The nursery is on this floor," he said, "and when I was a lad I spent many a rainy day gazing out this window."

In need of something that would distract her from imagining those firm lips finding their way down to hers, Isobel said, "Did you chant, 'Rain, rain, go away?' "

Her question made him chuckle. "Naturally, for what boy would choose to be indoors when he might be outside discovering the world?"

"None, I should imagine." As if unable to stop herself, Isobel looked up at him, fully aware that her expression might be thought provocative. "And what of now?" she asked. "Would you rather be outside at this moment?"

Robert's answer was to lower his head, allowing his lips to brush ever so lightly against hers. "At this moment," he said softly, "I am exactly where I wish to be. . . ."

Books by Martha Kirkland

THE GALLANT GAMBLER
THREE FOR BRIGHTON
THE NOBLE NEPHEW
THE SEDUCTIVE SPY
A GENTLEMAN'S DECEPTION

Published by Zebra Books

A GENTLEMAN'S DECEPTION

Martha Kirkland

Zebra Books
Kensington Publishing Corp.

http://www.zebrabooks.com

ZEBRA BOOKS are published by

Kensington Publishing Corp.
850 Third Avenue
New York, NY 10022

Zebra and the Z logo Reg. U.S. Pat. & TM Off.

First Printing: June, 1999
10 9 8 7 6 5 4 3 2 1

Printed in the United States of America

To Helena Carter Robisch, who knows the meaning of the word *friend*.

One

Honoring his word proved more difficult than Robert Montford had imagined. Unfortunately, it had never been more important that he keep his promise, for a woman's life depended upon his finding Fiona Cochran.

He had tried everything he knew to find Lady Baysworth's sister, beginning with the hiring of a dozen Bow Street Runners and paying them double their usual fee to work with all speed. The detectives had traveled from one end of the country to another, showing the miniature portrait of Fiona and asking questions of thespians in every theater company from London to Land's End. All they had discovered so far was that an actor calling himself Byron Smyth had contracted influenza during the epidemic of 1789 and was probably buried somewhere in a pauper's grave. Of the young girl who had eloped with Smyth twenty-five years ago, there was not a trace.

Though Bow Street promised to continue the search, time was running out. Robert's mother had informed him just that afternoon that Lady Baysworth, who was his godmother, was now refusing all sustenance. "If something is not done," Agatha Montford had said, her voice catching on a sob, "the dearest friend I ever had will not live beyond the week."

A man of action, Robert had found it difficult to sit passively while others searched for Fiona. For that reason, when he received a letter scarce two hours later informing him that one of the Runners had found an actress in Gresham who bore a definite resemblance to the miniature, he set out immediately for the prosperous market town. The well-sprung barouche covered the ten mile distance in just over an hour, and as the coachman halted the team outside The Gresham Theater, where an itinerant acting troupe was booked for the week, Robert spied the Runner leaning against the ticket seller's booth.

There was no mistaking the detective, for his red vest was in evidence beneath his dark green coat. Like the majority of Runners, he was built like an ox, and though he was several inches shorter than Robert's six feet, he was the sort of fellow prudent people took pains not to cross.

Wasting no time, Robert jumped down from the coach and approached the man. "I am Robert Montford," he said.

The Runner removed a silver toothpick from between his rather fleshy lips. "Jethro Comstock," he replied, tipping his beaver hat politely. "The young woman is h'inside the building now, sir. One of the actresses she be."

"Are you certain of her identity?"

The man shrugged his massive shoulders. "B'aint nothing certain, sir, save death and the grave."

Taking the caveat in good part, Robert said, "Then let us go inside and see this actress."

"A good idea," the Runner replied. "Trouble is, the bloke at the door won't let nobody backstage before the play commences."

Robert muttered an oath, impatient to see the woman for himself. "Did you tell the doorman we were here on a matter of importance?"

The Runner shrugged his shoulders again. "The bloke didn't seem h'impressed with the h'important nature of our mission. 'E said if we wanted to see the actress, we'd be obliged to purchase a ticket like everyone else, or wait until after the performance."

Not wanting to stand about for several hours, Robert purchased a box just off the stage, and without another word he and the Runner passed through the entrance doors and climbed the single set of stairs leading to the boxes. After Robert surrendered the ivory circular token, an usher led them to their seats and provided them with printed programs of the evening's entertainment.

Robert gave the program only a cursory glance. As he expected, the performance consisted of a drama, a farce, and a pantomime. The drama, Shakespeare's *The Merchant of Venice*, starred the company manager, Mr. Geofrey Ragsdale, as Shylock, and featured The Beautiful Miss Shirley Dees as Portia.

While Robert scanned the list of supporting players for the name Fiona Cochran, or even Fiona Smyth, the Runner said, "H'if you'll forgive my saying so, Mr. Montford, what you're doing, trying to save a lady what's dying of a broken 'eart, fair makes me think of a play."

"Except, of course," Robert replied, "that should Lady Baysworth succumb to her malaise, she will not rise up at the sound of applause and take a bow. To the contrary, she will pass forever from this world, and if that should happen, it will break my own mother's heart."

Recalled to his mission by the thought of his god-mother's steadily worsening condition and his mother's valiant attempt to save her friend, Robert tossed aside the printed program. Not a fancier of the theater at the best of times, he was in no mood to be entertained. With no thought but to bide his time until he could go backstage, he settled as comfortably as possible in the thinly padded chair, his arms folded across his chest, and prepared himself for what he suspected would be a rather amateurish exhibition. His suspicions proved accurate, for the players were every bit as unskilled as he had anticipated.

Geofrey Ragsdale, a rather portly individual, por-trayed Shylock in the old-fashioned mode, as a pure villain, complete with the red beard of Judas and an atrocious hooked nose. His acting ability was little better than his costume, and he shouted and pos-tured until the groundlings in the pit grew restless and began to boo and hiss.

Robert, impatient to be backstage, was about to take himself around to the rear of the theater to see if he could bribe the doorman into admitting him when Miss Shirley Dees appeared on stage. In the beginning of the scene her back was to Robert, but just as she uttered the lines, "I may neither choose whom I would, nor refuse whom I dislike; so is the will of a living daughter curbed by the will of a dead father," she turned to her right, giving Robert an unimpeded view of her face.

For a full minute, he could only stare, doubting the testimony of his eyes.

"There now," Comstock said. "Was I right to send for you, sir?"

Vouchsafing no reply, Robert gave his full attention to the stage, for not fifteen feet away from him stood a living, breathing facsimile of the miniature of Fiona Cochran. Hope warred with incredulity as Robert pulled the small portrait from his pocket to compare the two women. To his relief, his imagination had not played him false, for there was the same black hair, the same creamy skin, the same full, voluptuous lips.

The only thing that was not consistent with the painting was the age of the female. The girl in the portrait was just turned sixteen, while the actress before him was no longer in the first blush of youth. Of course, she was also not a woman of forty-two, the age Fiona would be at present. Robert guessed the young woman to be no more than twenty-three or twenty-four, and, though that made her too young to be Fiona Cochran, she could easily be Fiona's daughter.

Robert cared little who he found, the mother or the daughter. He would gladly take either or both of them to Montford House. In fact, he would cheerfully deliver an entire family of women, if by so doing he would restore Lady Baysworth's will to live.

Luckily, the play was a shortened version of the original *The Merchant of Venice*, and Robert was not obliged to sit through the entire five acts. Still, he was impatient to speak to Miss Shirley Dees. When the drama finally came to an end, he left the Runner to enjoy the remainder of the program while he hurried out the front of the building and around to the rear entrance. As he suspected, once he bribed the doorman with a guinea, he was directed to the actress's dressing room.

Despite the apparent order illuminated by the oil-powered footlights out front, behind the scenes everything was chaos and clutter. In the ill-lit corridors, scenery and stage props filled every available space, with smaller objects piled in corners, larger pieces leaning against the walls, and a hodgepodge of items stacked in wooden crates that reached almost to the low ceiling. As for the actors and actresses, they were obliged to make their costume changes in whatever niches were left.

Robert found the play's female lead in what amounted to a large closet equipped with a rickety wooden chair and a small table. Upon the table reposed a small lamp, a hand-held looking glass, a comb and brush, a tray of rouge and cream pots, and a wire wig form. If there had ever been a door to the so-called dressing room it had been removed, and in its place a faded curtain had been nailed across the opening to provide some degree of privacy.

Because there was little air circulating, the actress had pushed the curtain aside. She had already removed the costume she had worn as Portia in the final scene, exchanging it for a flannel wrapper tied loosely at the waist, but Robert had no difficulty in recognizing her. Even taking into consideration her kohl-lined eyes and the rouged cheeks and lips, she still resembled the miniature of Fiona.

"Miss Dees?"

"I am sorry," she said, her voice cool and brooking no contradiction, "but I do not mingle with the audience. Please return to your seat."

"You misunderstand my purpose, madam, for I have not come to—"

"I understand well enough, sir. You are not the first man to buy his way backstage, and I doubt you will be the last. I tell you as I tell them all: you paid for a play, and you got a play. Now be so good as to step away."

She was already reaching for the curtain when Robert caught her wrist. "Not so fast."

To his surprise, she did not struggle to break free, though her blue eyes blazed with anger. "Unhand me this instant."

"Directly," he said. "You have nothing to fear from me, but I must speak with you. I have come on an important errand, and I will not be gainsaid. A lady of my acquaintance is quite ill, and I am searching for her sister, a woman named Fiona Cochran." He paid close attention to the actress's face as he spoke. Her expression revealed nothing save her continued anger. "Does that name mean anything to you?"

"No," she said. "I never heard it before."

Aware that actors often used aliases, he said, "What of Byron Smyth? Surely you knew him."

She shook her head. "I have no knowledge of such a person."

"Are you quite certain?"

"Quite," she replied, staring pointedly at the fingers still gripping her wrist. "Now, if you do not let go of my arm this instant, I promise you I will scream. The troupe manager employs a rather large individual who takes pleasure in tossing unauthorized visitors into the street. I am persuaded you will enjoy making his acquaintance even less than I have enjoyed making yours."

Robert released her wrist, but he did not accept his dismissal. "Miss Dees, it is imperative that I find—"

"I am not Shirley Dees," she said.

"Do not take me for a fool, young woman. Your name is on the playbill, and—"

"I am the understudy. Whenever the principal actress is . . . er . . . unwell, I fill in for her. To cut down on expenses, the playbills are never changed."

Damn the Runner! He might have told me this woman's name!

"If you wish to speak with Miss Dees," she continued, "I suggest you go to The Belled Cat. It is the inn just down the street. Perhaps she will have recovered sufficiently from her indisposition to be able to answer your questions."

Deciding the understudy's name was of no consequence, Robert said, "I no longer wish to speak with the star. Whatever you call yourself, it is you to whom I—"

"I have no time for this. In less than five minutes, the manager will expect me to be standing center stage, suitably costumed for the pantomime. Therefore, I must insist you leave me alone."

Having made her wishes clear, she reached up and yanked the curtain down. Though Robert did not interfere this time, allowing the thick material to fall between them, he merely stepped back several paces. He had no intention of leaving the building, not before he had discovered a great deal more about the young woman. It was unimportant what alias she chose to use. What mattered to Robert was not her name, but her face—a face that looked so much like the one in the miniature that it could not be a coincidence.

Deciding to make it perfectly clear to her that he would be waiting when the pantomime was finished, he pushed aside the curtain. To his surprise, the actress had removed the flannel wrapper and tossed it across the back of the wooden chair, and she was at that moment reaching for a gaudy jonquil and turquoise striped taffeta costume that hung from a peg on the wall.

Robert stared unashamedly, for her slim, yet tantalizingly rounded figure was covered only by a lawn shift that had been sewn to fit snugly at the narrow curve of her waist—a shift that succeeded in revealing almost as much as it concealed. The woman was a beauty—no doubt about it!

Following very natural instincts, Robert let his attention settle first upon her bare shoulders. Then he allowed his gaze to travel lower, to the full swell of her breasts, his view only slightly obstructed by the thin material of the shift. Captivated by what he saw and momentarily diverted by the stirring in his blood, he took several seconds before he managed to lift his eyes to her face. There he received an even greater surprise, for along with her wrapper the actress had dispensed with Portia's black hair, which now adorned the wire wig form on the table.

Trailing down the woman's back was a single thick plait of reddish blond hair, and without the black wig her resemblance to Fiona Cochran was not nearly so pronounced. Actually, with the exception of the blue eyes and the full lips, the similarity between the actress and the girl in the miniature was now superficial at best.

The young woman's face had turned pink with embarrassment, and only after she had covered her partially exposed bosom with the striped taffeta—a costume suitable for Columbine, Harlequin's love— was she able to speak. "How . . . how dare you! I warned you that I would scream."

Still reeling from the discovery that the actress was not a brunette, Robert stepped back and made her a formal bow. "I ask your pardon, miss. I did not mean to—"

"Get out!"

"As you wish, madam."

He bowed a second time, let the curtain fall between them, then turned and strode purposefully toward the exit door. Disappointment accompanied his every step, for it had all been an illusion. Of course, that was what the theater was all about, make-believe, but he could not help feeling disheartened after the earlier elation of thinking he had found Fiona's daughter.

Muttering something to the doorman, who bid him a good evening, Robert stepped out into the high street. After pausing a minute or two to collect his thoughts and attempt to curb his growing frustration, he signaled to his coachman, who waited with a group of other drivers just down the way.

The servant came immediately. "Yes, sir," he said, touching his forelock respectfully. "Shall I bring the carriage around, sir?"

"No. Take me to it. A walk in the night air may be just what I need to clear my head."

As they passed the front entrance to the theater

someone opened the door, and Robert heard a soprano singing of her love for the clown, Harlequin. The voice was unexpectedly lovely, and as clear and pure as the first snowfall of winter. Even if Robert had not gotten a glimpse of the Columbine costume, he felt certain he would have known the voice belonged to the young understudy. On a whim, he gave the ticket taker a shilling to let him step inside for the duration of the song.

The audience was spellbound. Even the groundlings sat quietly on their rows of wooden benches, their attention riveted to the stage and the captivating Columbine. At that distance, the jonquil and turquoise stripes did not look at all gaudy, but Robert was obliged to admit that the talent and beauty of the young woman may have been partially responsible for his revised opinion of the costume.

At that moment, she chanced to turn his way, and—though at such a distance Robert was certain he was just another face in the crowd—she seemed to be looking directly at him. He stood very still, watching her and listening to her sweet, warm voice, and for that brief interlude he felt as though she sang not of her love for some fictional character, but of a real love—a love that had existed from the beginning of time. In that instant, Robert fancied it was to him she sang, that it was he she loved.

Feeling like one bewitched, he shook his head as if to clear it of such foolish imagination. She was an actress, a spinner of dreams, and she was probably having a similar effect upon every male in the audience.

As Columbine she wore her hair loose, and the reddish blond tresses swung free about her shoulders, making her look more like a girl of sixteen than a woman grown. He knew it was an illusion, for he had seen her only minutes earlier, a woman fully seven years older than the character she portrayed. She was a skilled actress, he would give her that, and more than capable of weaving a spell.

No longer under that spell, he lamented the existence of the blond hair. Considering her slight facial resemblance to the girl in the miniature, with the dark wig and a little of that stage magic she might have been able to convince Lady Baysworth that she was her niece.

Robert had no more begun that thought than he knew exactly what he meant to do. It was a rash plan—perhaps even an underhanded one—but when he weighed the ethics of a bit of playacting against the possible loss of a woman's life, he dismissed any qualms he might ordinarily have felt.

"Excuse me," he whispered to the ticket taker, "do you know the name of the actress playing Columbine? Her real name?"

"That I do, guv."

As he watched Robert remove a guinea from his waistcoat pocket, a smile split the man's face. "The name is Townsend," he said, tucking the gold coin inside his right glove. "Isobel Townsend."

"*Miss* Townsend?"

"As to that, sir, I couldn't rightly say. But I ain't never seen no husband, if that's what you're wishful of knowing. Nor any gentlemen callers, for that matter, though there be many as would be happy to fill the bill." His smile turned to a leer. "You thinking of trying your luck, guv?"

Robert ignored the question. "And she is residing at . . . ?"

The man hesitated until Robert produced another coin, then looked about him to make certain he was not overheard. "The entire troupe is staying at The Belled Cat. It is just down the street there, on the right. You go past the—"

"Never mind," Robert said, already turning toward the door. "I know the way."

It lacked but a few minutes to midnight when Isobel heard the thick stage door close behind her. As usual, she was the last of the company to leave the theater, for unlike most of the members of the acting troupe she adhered to a strict regimen of makeup removal. Since she hoped to escape the pitted complexion of the average thespian, it was her practice not only to avoid the lead and mercury based makeups, but also to wash her face thoroughly after each performance. After every last sign of rouge, kohl, and powder were gone, she always applied a light coating of a balm of Gilead that she prepared herself. Because of her fidelity to this regimen, her skin was still clear and smooth, even after five years on the stage.

Once in the high street, she breathed deeply of the cool night air. After the close quarters backstage, it was always a relief to come outside. The sky was clear and filled almost to overflowing with bright, silvery stars, and the moon was full, shining enough light upon the cobbled street to remove any danger that a person might trip and fall.

For a woman alone there were other dangers, of course, so as Isobel turned to her right, her destination The Belled Cat, she traveled at a brisk pace. As she hurried toward the old, gray stone inn, the hem of her long, dark blue cloak billowing out behind her, she recalled the man who had intruded upon her privacy. She must remember to tell Mr. Ragsdale about the incident, for those backstage lotharios were becoming a nuisance. This one had very nearly caused her to be late for Columbine's entrance.

Except for the persistence of the tall stranger, and the embarrassment of being caught clothed in nothing but her shift, it had been a good night. While she was on stage everything had gone perfectly, and the audience had been uncommonly appreciative of the performances, especially Isobel's, bringing her back for three curtain calls following the pantomime. Almost an hour later, Isobel still felt that exhilaration that was so difficult to explain to someone who had never performed. With the memory of her success filling her thoughts, she was surprised into a gasp when a man suddenly leapt from a waiting coach and stepped directly in front of her, blocking her path.

"Please move aside," she said, trying to disguise the alarm she felt. "I should like to pass."

"Miss Townsend," the man said, "forgive me if I startled you, but I must speak with you upon a matter of importance. Time is of the essence, and I know you and the acting company leave after tomorrow's performance. Therefore, I—"

"You! Sir, I told you I am not the person you seek."

"And I accept your word upon the subject. Be that as it may—"

"If you believe me, then why do you persist in harassing me?"

He had the audacity to smile, as though theirs was

a meeting welcome to the two of them. "Actually, madam, it is a matter of logistics. Fiona Cochran is not here, and you are. Therefore, I have decided that you will do well enough for what I have in mind."

"Do well enough for . . ." She sputtered to a stop. How dared he! Outrage and apprehension warred inside Isobel, and she pulled her cloak close around her, as if for protection. She was aware that the general public considered actresses little better than prostitutes plying their trade, but until this moment she had never been accosted on the street by someone wishing to proposition her. And with so little finesse!

"Get out of my way!"

He did not move. "I fear I cannot, madam."

"Of course you can. You have but to take two steps in either direction, and—"

"I will make it worth your time," he said. "I ask only that you come to my home for an hour or so, and for this you may name your price. A week's wages. Two weeks' wages."

Isobel's palm itched to slap his face. Anger had begun to triumph over fear, and she wished she dared land the libertine a facer. Fortunately, her instinct for self-preservation stilled those combatant impulses, for the man was too tall and much too muscular. Furthermore, she had firsthand knowledge of his strength, for when last she had looked, her wrist still bore the mark of his fingers.

"Well, madam? What say you?"

She tried to remain calm, but when she spoke she could not keep the indignation from her voice. "I say only what I said before. Get out of my way!"

Still he did not move, and when he spoke, his

voice was incredulous. "You cannot mean to refuse me out of hand."

"That is exactly what I mean to do. Now, move aside, or I shall—"

"But it is a simple task I ask of you, and surely one you have done hundreds of times before. Can you not reconsider?"

"Hundreds of . . . Why, you . . . you . . ." She could not think of a name vile enough to call him, and the feeling of impotence only fueled her anger. When he reached out a hand, as if to take her by the arm, Isobel lifted her booted foot and brought it down hard upon his instep. Since he was dressed for the evening, his footwear consisted of low-cut pumps—shoes with little protection—and he cried out in surprise and apparent discomfort.

"Damnation, woman!"

While he looked down at his injured foot, Isobel seized the opportunity to step around him. Once past him, she began to run toward the inn, the back of her cloak billowing out behind her as she fled.

"Damnation!" he said again. Then, on the instant, she heard his footfalls sounding loud upon the cobbled street. He was in pursuit, and Isobel knew she must hurry, for with his longer legs he would soon overtake her.

Fear made her run as she had never run before. She had only just reached the entrance to the inn yard and was about to pass beneath the swinging sign featuring a large cat with a bell around its neck when she felt a powerful tug on her cloak. Because the clasp at the neck was securely fastened it all but choked her, and she was stopped in her tracks. Before she knew what was happening, she felt the fullness of the cloak being tossed over her head like a sack.

She would have fallen to her knees if a strong arm had not caught her around the waist and lifted her off her feet. As she drew breath to scream, she felt a hand clamp over her mouth, effectively silencing her. She tried to fight her captor, but with the cloak wrapped around her, her arms were pinned to her side. She kicked and squirmed with all her might, to no avail. To her horror, the man shifted her weight around to his side and carried her like a sack of wheat back down the street.

No more than a minute later, an astonished male voice protested from somewhere above her. "Sir! What be the meaning of—"

"No questions," her captor said. Then he tossed her into a carriage. "To Montford House," he ordered.

"But, sir, this be highly irreg—"

"Go!" he yelled, his tone brooking no disobedience.

Immediately, Isobel felt the coach sway as the man jumped in beside her and slammed the door. Seconds later a whip cracked over the heads of the team and the coach lurched forward, rattling noisily over the stones of the empty street. To Isobel's horror, within a matter of minutes they had left the village and were on the smoother surface of the road.

She had no idea where she was bound, nor when or if she would be returned. Of only two things was she certain—whatever this madman had in mind for her to do, she would not do it willingly, and somehow she would make him rue the day he had kidnapped Isobel Townsend.

Two

"Believe me, madam, this is all your doing."

"Mine!"

"Absolutely, for you would not listen to reason."

Isobel had fought free of the cloak that imprisoned her, and now she pushed back against the buttery soft leather squabs of the coach, her objective to get as far away from this lunatic as possible. "*I* would not listen to reason? The accusation sits ill upon your lips, sir, for you are obviously demented. There can be no other explanation for your actions—actions, I might add, for which you will pay dearly!"

"I expect to do so. Did I not tell you that you could name your own price?"

She stiffened. "I meant that you would be deported. You cannot kidnap a lady off the street without paying the consequences."

"What foolishness is this? I assure you, madam, you have not been kidnapped."

The audacity of the man! "Perhaps it is an accepted practice here in the wilds of Norfolk to chase females down the street, maul them about, then toss them into a waiting coach and whisk them away to heaven knows where, but in London such behavior is called abduction. And though you may find this difficult to believe, the courts frown upon such conduct."

He was silent for several moments. "If I mauled you about, as you put it, I offer you my apologies. Unfortunately, desperate circumstances call for desperate measures." The apology obviously at an end, he added, "Besides, it was you who resorted to violence. I am persuaded at least one of my toes is broken."

"Good! As you said, 'Desperate circumstances call for desperate measures.' When I am threatened, I do what I must to protect myself."

"But I offered you no threat, madam. As I told you, I merely wished to speak with you."

"Ah, yes, how foolish of me to misinterpret your intentions. The next time a complete stranger waits in the shadows and then jumps out at me, blocking my way and making all manner of lewd proposals, I will remind myself that he merely wishes *to speak with me.*"

Robert was almost as surprised by her accusation as he had been by the quite harsh abuse of his foot. When he looked at her, however, huddled in the corner of the coach and regarding him much as one might a mad dog poised to spring, he decided she believed what she said. "I made you no proposals, Miss Townsend, lewd or otherwise. I wished to hire you."

"So you said. For an hour or two. At your home." Her voice now had a defensive edge to it. "I am aware of the opinion held by many that actresses are for sale to the highest bidder, but I assure you, that belief is more fantasy than fact."

As she threw his words back at him, Robert realized how easily they could have been misinterpreted, especially by the sort of woman who must receive propositions on a regular basis. "This is all a misunderstanding. I wish to engage your services as an actress. Nothing more."

When she made no reply, he said, "I believe I told you backstage that an acquaintance of mine is gravely ill. The lady is my godmother, and my mother's dearest friend. She has recently suffered the loss of both her husband and Gordon, her only son—the one in a carriage accident, and the other while fighting in the Peninsula—and now she feels herself alone in the world, without a reason to live."

Miss Townsend said nothing, but at least she had relaxed, no longer attempting to push her way through the squabs of his coach.

"When I saw you tonight," he continued, "dressed as Portia and wearing the black wig, your resemblance to the lady's sister was pronounced. I cannot tell you how hopeful I was that you might prove to be Fiona Cochran's daughter."

"I do not remember my mother," she said quietly, "but I am certain of her name. It was Mary. When my father was alive, he often told me I looked like her."

"As luck would have it, you also resemble the lady I seek. Of course, when I saw you without the wig, I realized your likeness to Fiona was only superficial, and at that moment I was quite prepared to leave without another word to you."

"You should have done so, for it was a much better plan than this . . . this idiocy." After that sharp retort, she remained silent for a time. Finally, in the strained silence, she said, "Since you obviously did not leave as you had planned, what changed your mind?"

"You did. Or more accurately, the spell you cast over the audience when you sang as Columbine. You had at least two hundred people believing you were a lovesick girl of sixteen. Watching you, I was almost convinced that you—" He stopped short, for he had very nearly told her of his feeling that she sang to him alone. Not wishing to divulge that flight of fancy, he said, "Watching you mesmerize the audience, I knew you could perform a similar magic upon my godmother, and I asked myself what would be the harm in making Lady Baysworth believe you might be her niece."

"For one thing," she said, "it would be a falsehood. For another, if the lady is as ill as you say, I believe it would be a cruel deception."

"Perhaps, but if my godmother continues to refuse food, she will not see the end of the week. That, I am persuaded, would be a far greater cruelty than any deception of my devising. Besides, as an actress, you pretend all the time. What difference can it make if you enact one more role?"

"It would make a difference to me. When I act upon the stage, all those who see me know it is make-believe. What you would have me do is deceit, and I abhor nothing so much as a falsehood."

Robert could not credit her words. "Come now, Miss Townsend, we all fib a little now and then. Civilization as we know it would crumble if everyone went around telling the absolute truth. Only consider the consequences of asking a simple, 'How are you?' "

She did not smile as he had hoped. "Civilization notwithstanding, sir, I always tell the truth."

"Always?"

"Always."

In the face of such insistence, he abandoned his hope that she might accept fifty pounds to pretend to be Fiona's daughter. Unwilling to give up, however, he said, "How about this, then? Simply come to visit Lady Baysworth. You need say nothing, merely allow her to look at you and draw her own conclusions as to your identity."

She shook her head. "That would still be a lie, albeit by omission. My answer is the same. I will not do it."

Exasperated, Robert swallowed an oath. "On the contrary, madam, you will. As you pointed out, I have already abducted you, so what can it matter if I compounded the offense by carrying you bound and gagged up to her ladyship's bedchamber?"

"You would not dare!"

"Do not wager your last groat on that assumption, for you will lose. Actually, it is not a bad idea, your being bound and gagged. If you were rendered immobile, my godmother could look at you to her heart's content, and you would be unable to deny any relationship to her sister."

The coachman slowed the carriage, alerting Robert to the fact that they had reached the lane and the low flint wall that ran for perhaps a mile, ending at the estate entrance. Within minutes, the team turned left and passed between the dignified red brick columns that stood on either side of the wrought iron gates. Like the columns, the Palladian-style house was fashioned of red brick, and though

Robert could not see his home from that spot he knew it waited at the end of the crushed rock carriageway, its symmetrical lines softened by the silvery white moonlight.

He heard the crunch of gravel beneath the wheels as they traveled the final quarter mile to the house. His guest heard it too, for she sat up straight, eyeing the carriage door as though she contemplated throwing it open and jumping to the ground.

"I advise against it," he said, relaxing against the squabs as though he had not a care in the world. "Such foolish heroics would achieve nothing, and might well result in a broken leg. And should you escape me, your success would be short-lived, for you are on my estate now, and no one who lives here would defy me by giving you aid. You might just as well do as I say, Miss Townsend, for there is not one person to whom you may turn for help."

In this, however, Robert was mistaken. He had reckoned without Agatha Montford, who had spent the evening sitting with Lady Baysworth, trying to will some of her own strength into her friend's frail body. His mother had only just quit the sickroom when she very nearly bumped into her son, who ushered an obviously reluctant guest up the broad staircase.

"Robert!" she said, shock writ plainly upon her face. "What is the meaning of this?"

Her son's answer did not come until they were seated in the pale blue sitting room that adjoined the lady's bedchamber. Once the butler had brought a simple tea tray and bowed himself out, Robert told his mother about his hope that Isobel would agree to impersonate Fiona's daughter.

"I told him I would not do it," Isobel said, setting aside the teacup from which she had taken only a sip of the dark, fragrant brew. "You have my sincerest sympathy, Mrs. Montford, for it cannot be easy to watch the steady decline in a friend's health. However, I will not be a party to deceiving her."

Robert Montford muttered something beneath his breath, then downed a somewhat stronger drink than tea. Once the glass was empty, he set it on the pink-veined marble mantel in a manner guaranteed to render the delicate crystal unusable in the future. "Madam, you are the most obstinate woman it has ever been my displeasure to know."

"Robert, please," his mother said. "Miss Townsend is a guest in our home, albeit a less than enthusiastic one, and I should dislike it of all things if she returned to the village loathing all of Norfolk because of our lack of hospitality."

The lady looked directly at Isobel then, caution battling with hope in her hazel eyes. "I wish we had not started off on the wrong footing, my dear, for though I abhor the tactics my son employed to bring you here, I cannot in all truth say I am disappointed to meet you."

The words were nicely phrased, but Isobel was not so foolish as to misinterpret them as a compliment to herself. Agatha Montford, like her son, wanted to make use of the resemblance between Isobel and her friend's missing sister. The lady's wish was written all over her still pretty face. Being the mother of Robert Montford, she was obliged to be close to fifty years old, yet she retained a quite youthful appearance and a genuinely kind expression—an expression marred only by the obvious sadness that weighed upon her heart.

"Mrs. Montford," Isobel said, wishing to make her position quite clear, "I appreciate your desire to do all within your power to help your friend, but—"

"A moment," she said, holding up her hand to silence Isobel before she could reject the plan. "Perhaps we might speak more freely if we were alone. Conversing woman-to-woman, as it were." Turning toward her son, she asked him if he would be so kind as to look in on Lady Baysworth, to discover if she was asleep.

For a moment, Isobel thought he might refuse, for the set of his jaw was determined, to say the least. He must have thought better of his mother's suggestion, however, for he inclined his head slightly. "Perhaps you are right, ma'am. Miss Townsend would not see reason when I explained what was needed, but if you think a woman's touch will help persuade her to cooperate, I will give you all the privacy you wish."

As he quit the room, he cast one last exasperated look in Isobel's direction. Not about to be intimidated by him, Isobel gave him stare for stare, yet when he had closed the door behind him she spared a moment to wonder how that handsome face might look should the man allow a smile to play upon his lips.

"Now, my dear," Agatha Montford began the moment they were alone, "let me make it clear that I sympathize completely with your unwillingness to go against your principles. Your scruples do you credit."

"However . . ." Isobel interjected, knowing full well the word was but a breath away.

"However," the lady continued, undeterred by Isobel's awareness of her plan, "many of us do things we would really rather not do, especially when such an act will benefit those in need of our assistance."

"But, I—"

"For just such an example, I am persuaded that one need look no farther than my son."

Isobel only just stopped herself from scoffing. Robert Montford was the most arrogant, domineering man she had ever had the misfortune to encounter, and if he had ever done anything he did not wish to do, she would eat her best straw bonnet.

"I was widowed a dozen years ago," her hostess continued, "and upon the death of my husband, my son—who had just completed his first year at Oxford—inherited an encumbered estate and a mountain of debts incurred by his father." She paused and took several sips of her tea, as though it was thirsty work telling such intimate details about her family.

"You must know that Robert had never really been interested in managing the estate. From childhood it had been his dearest wish to become a scientist. Science was his passion, and though he enjoyed sports and the company of his friends he gave the majority of his attention to preparing himself for a life of scientific discovery."

"I see," Isobel said. The words were said out of mere politeness; actually, she did not see what any of this had to do with her. Furthermore, Robert Montford had wealth, power, and uncommon good looks; she saw no reason to waste any sympathy on him.

Apparently Mrs. Montford read her thoughts, for she hurried to continue with her story. "You may imagine my son's disappointment when, at the tender age of eighteen, he was obliged to abandon his hope of a scientific career and return to Norfolk to see what he could do to reclaim the estate. The welfare of more than twenty-five tenant families depended upon his doing the job and doing it well. So, when the situation was explained to him, Robert left the university. Without a word, he sacrificed his dreams for the good of the estate and those who live on it."

Isobel was not unacquainted with sacrifice and the disappointment that accompanied it, for her own father had returned to the stage in order to pay for her schooling. For some reason, Thomas Townsend had insisted that Isobel receive an education befitting a young lady. Unfortunately, his sacrifice had kept him and his only child apart for the remaining years of his life—years that were, for a young girl, filled with loneliness.

Feeling more in sympathy with Robert Montford, and interested in spite of her dislike of the man who had brought her here, Isobel bid his mother continue her story.

"In the years that followed," she said, a touch of pride in her voice, "never once did I hear my son complain at the forced abandonment of his goals. He accepted the role he had thought would not fall to him for another thirty years, and he brought the estate back into full productivity. Through his unselfishness, he assured the continued health and happiness of upwards of one hundred people."

Agatha Montford put her teacup on the small table beside her pale blue slipper chair and leaned forward to take Isobel's hands in hers. "I ask no such sacrifice of you, my dear, and under no circumstances do I wish you to abandon your scruples. I ask only that you allow me to take you to see a woman whose heart is broken."

While Isobel sat helplessly, her hands held tightly, Agatha Montford's eyes filled with moisture. Then slowly, silently, tears slid down the lady's cheeks. As an actress, Isobel had been on stage with numerous fellow thespians who could produce copious tears on cue. These tears were different. They were not the product of a learned craft, but the result of a deep and sincere love of one friend for another.

Isobel had never known that kind of friendship, and in spite of her resolve not to be swayed something deep inside her was stirred by the lady's devotion. As if sensing the fact that she was weakening, Agatha Montford pressed her to reconsider her position."Please, my dear, could you not see your way clear to do this one little thing for my friend?"

Though Isobel was quite certain she never gave her consent to visit the sickroom, scarce five minutes later she found herself being ushered into that very bedchamber. A brace of candles burned on the fruit-wood table beside the massive, canopied bed, and beneath the pale yellow counterpane lay a woman whose frailness was evident even from the doorway.

Robert Montford sat in a Queen Anne chair pulled up close to the bed, but at their entrance he stood and moved the chair out of the way. If he was surprised to see Isobel, he gave no indication of the fact.

"Edith," Agatha Montford said, holding Isobel's hand in a grasp that threatened to cut off the circulation of blood to her fingers, "someone has come to see you." She crossed the room, pulling Isobel in her wake, not stopping until she was quite near the bed. "Open your eyes, Edith, and look at your visitor."

At that moment, Isobel would have given her immortal soul to be anyplace but in that room. She wanted no part of it, yet there she was, standing at the bedside of a complete stranger, watching as the woman's paper-thin eyelids slowly lifted to reveal lackluster eyes.

In that first instant, Lady Baysworth gazed at Isobel as though she cared little who her visitor might be. Within a matter of seconds, however, the lackluster had vanished, replaced by a brightness that was almost feverish—one part disbelief, one part hope. "Fiona?" she said, her voice little more than a whisper. "Is that . . . can it be you?"

Isobel had never felt so wretched. She wanted to give the invalid hope, yet she could not make herself utter the falsehood. "I am sorry," she said, the words catching in her throat and all but choking her, "but I am not Fiona."

"Of course she is not," Agatha Montford said, apparently not put off in the least by Isobel's reply. "She is much too young to be Fiona." Then, lowering her voice in a manner that gave the words added significance, she said, "Robert met the young lady at The Gresham Theater. She is an actress."

A tinge of color showed in Lady Baysworth's pale face. "An actress, did you say?"

"I did, indeed. If you will, Edith, look at her closely. Tell me what you think."

Her ladyship did as she was bid, not taking her attention from Isobel's face. "Is she . . . Oh, Agatha, could she be Fiona's daughter?"

"She insists that she is not," Agatha Montford replied, but her words lacked conviction. After lifting the brace of candles so they illuminated Isobel's features, she gave her a little nudge toward the bed. "Move closer, my dear, so Edith can have a proper look at you."

With great reluctance, Isobel took another step nearer to the woman, who had not ceased to stare at her. "Now, my dear," Mrs. Montford said, "be so good as to introduce yourself to Lady Baysworth."

Isobel, relieved that she had not been asked to tell an untruth, curtsied politely and offered her hand to the invalid. "How do you do, ma'am. My name is Isobel Townsend."

Her ladyship's lower lip began to tremble. "What did you say?"

"Miss Townsend's name is Isobel," Agatha Montford answered, her tone one of triumph. "*Mary* Isobel, to be precise."

To Isobel's horror, Lady Baysworth caught her hand, but instead of shaking it politely she lifted it to her lips, placing a fevered kiss upon Isobel's skin. "My dear, dear child," she said, hugging the captured hand to her cheek as though she meant to never let it go, "I had no idea of your existence."

Mortified, Isobel tried to disengage her hand.

"Lady Baysworth, I fear there has been a mistake. I am not your niece."

Her ladyship was not listening. Instead, she looked toward her friend. "Bless you for this, Agatha. And bless Fiona, too, for she did not, after all, forget her family."

"Your ladyship," Isobel said, still trying to free herself from the lady's surprisingly determined grasp, "please, you must listen to me. I am sorry to be the instrument of your further pain, but I am *not* Fiona's child."

"But of course you are," the invalid insisted, her face radiant. "Otherwise, why would you be named Mary Isobel, after our mother?"

Three

"It is nothing more than coincidence," Isobel said. "Pure happenstance."

Robert Montford made no reply. He merely leaned back against the squabs of the coach, and while the carriage rolled along, his brown eyes searched her face. For most of the return journey to the market town of Gresham he had stared at her, as if by the sheer intensity of his gaze he might discover the truth of the matter.

"Neither of my names is at all uncommon," she said. "One might meet an Isobel most any day of the week, and as for Marys, why there is one in every other household." She knew she was babbling, but it had been a long, emotionally draining night, and she found his continued silence unnerving.

"The combination of the two is, I admit, slightly less common," she continued, "but anyone might choose such a pairing. It does not make me Fiona Cochran's daughter. I am the child of Mary and Thomas Townsend."

The man opposite her still said nothing.

"Believe me, a person knows her own parents."

"Nevertheless," he said, speaking at last, "I want

your assurance that you will return to visit my god-mother before you leave the neighborhood."

"I told Lady Baysworth that I would return, and I will. I never—"

"Yes, I know," he said, his tone brusque. "You never lie."

"No," she said, her teeth clenched in annoyance, "I do not." She knew a strong desire to wring his neck, and she only just resisted the temptation to reach across the short distance that separated them. How dared he act impatient with her!

He had not been kidnapped off the street and dragged against his will to meet a woman he had never seen before. *He* had not stood before the invalid declaring his true identity, all the while knowing that one small deviation from *his* principles might well restore the woman to health.

If anyone had a right to be short-tempered, it was Isobel. Judging by the brightness of the sun that warmed the interior of the coach, it was already mid-morning, and she was exhausted. In addition to the distress she felt as a result of confronting Lady Baysworth, Isobel had found little opportunity for sleep.

After trying every bit of logic she could call to mind to convince the lady that she was not, indeed, the child of her long-lost sister—logic that made no impression whatever upon an opinion fueled by emotions—Isobel had spent the remainder of the night sitting in the rosewood Queen Anne chair Robert Montford pulled up to the bed for her. Lady Baysworth had added further to Isobel's discomfort by refusing to surrender her hand. Their fingers entwined, the invalid had held tightly to Isobel until just before dawn, when she fell into a restful sleep.

At some point, Isobel had nodded off for a brief period, but her repose was anything but restful. Furthermore, when she awoke this morning her neck was stiff, and she felt as if the curved back of the chair had become fused to her spine.

"You will not go?" Lady Baysworth had begged when Isobel stood to stretch out the kinks in her vertebra. "Promise me you will not!"

"Of course she will not," Agatha Montford answered for her, "but you must first make a promise of your own, my friend. Kendrick is bringing up a tray, and you must promise to eat something."

"I will," she said, "if Isobel will stay with me just a bit longer."

Unable to withstand the combined pressure from the two friends, Isobel had sat back down. "I will remain while you eat, Lady Baysworth, but as soon as you finish, I must return to the village. I am under contract to Geofrey Ragsdale, and I must honor my word."

When tears began to pool in her ladyship's eyes, Isobel added, "But if Mrs. Montford will send the carriage for me after this evening's performance, I will return for another visit with you before the troupe travels to Norwich for our next engagement."

With that the ladies had to be satisfied, for Isobel had meant what she said about not remaining at Montford House. "I am contracted to the Ragsdale troupe through the end of July, and after that, I have agreed to portray Columbine at The Haymarket Theater in London."

She had spoken with an understandable degree of pride, for it was a feather in her cap to earn a featured role at a London theater, but she had not been surprised when her auditors merely stared blankly at one another. For those two ladies, accustomed to every luxury life had to offer, the idea of appearing on any stage was an embarrassment. They would never understand that Isobel was proud of her work, and thankful she had a talent that allowed her to support herself.

Though she had been educated in a respectable female academy, Isobel's rather unyielding temperament rendered her unsuitable to be a governess or a lady's companion. Between those two choices and the possibility of going into service or becoming a ward of the parish, there were only two other alternatives: marriage, and the stage. She had not, of course, received any offers for her hand, for without a dowry she was as unlikely to receive a marriage proposal as she was to be invited to fly to the moon. Therefore, she had chosen the stage as her profession.

"We are almost there," Robert Montford said, bringing her thoughts back to the present.

"What?"

"Gresham," he said, though the sudden bump and rattle of the carriage wheels over the cobblestone streets clearly signaled their arrival in the village.

Within two or three minutes the coachman reined in the pair before the swinging sign of The Belled Cat, and when Robert chanced to glance toward the entrance to the rambling, old, gray stone building with its reed-thatched roof, he spied Jethro Comstock, the Bow Street Runner who had met him the night before. The fellow stood in the narrow doorway, deep in conversation with someone—a gentleman from the looks of his clothing, though Robert could not see the man's face.

Robert would not have given the pair a second thought if the Runner had not spied him as well, then acted as though he had been caught with his hand in the cookie jar. Moving quickly, Comstock had stepped in front of his companion, using his broad back to shield the man from view. In the next instant, the stranger had ducked into the inn, leaving the detective alone in the doorway.

"Something is amiss," Miss Townsend said, and before Robert knew what she meant by the remark, she had slipped across the carriage seat, opened the door for herself, and jumped to the ground.

Only then did Robert notice that upwards of a dozen people were gathered in the inn yard, standing in small groups and talking among themselves in a manner that was decidedly agitated. He recognized one or two of the actors who had appeared on stage the evening before, so it did not require any special shrewdness on his part to suppose the entire gathering were members of the Ragsdale troupe.

To Robert, the only thing noteworthy about the scene was that so many of the actors were up and about at this hour, for he had it on good authority that theater people usually remained abed until afternoon. However, his companion did not share his view of the matter; she obviously found the fact of their being abroad so early in the day disturbing enough to send her running to the nearest group.

"Oh, Miss Townsend," a rather insipid fellow said when he spied her approaching them, "have you heard the news? Of course you have not, for you have only just arrived. It is quite dreadful! And what we are to do, I cannot even imagine."

"Calm yourself," she bid him, "and tell me what has happened."

Robert alit from the coach, but he remained beside the vehicle, for he did not imagine his presence was wanted by any member of the group. While he stood quietly, he observed Miss Townsend as she moved over to the next group and listened to them with every sign of interest.

"Mr. Montford," Jethro Comstock called as he strolled toward Robert, acting for all the world as though he had only just noticed the coach and its owner. "Good day to you, sir."

"Comstock," Robert replied as the detective removed the ever-present silver toothpick from between his fleshy lips.

"Strange doings 'ere, sir."

Purposely showing little interest in the to-do in the inn yard, Robert said, "How so?"

"Well, sir, seems the manager of the acting troupe 'as absconded with all the earnings, leaving the actors without a groat to their names."

Robert cast a momentary look in Miss Townsend's direction, before returning his attention to the Runner, all pretense of disinterest gone. "When did this occur?"

"Near as I can discover, the bloke—Ragsdale, that is—snuck out sometime after midnight. Owed the inn, 'e did, and every last man and woman in the company. The owner of the theater is fit to be tied, and 'e's 'olding the play scenery until 'e receives the rental money promised 'im."

"Oh, dear, oh, dear," a thin, sallow-faced woman wailed, "what is to become of us?" The question was obviously rhetorical, for no one vouchsafed an answer, and the woman turned her head into the shoulder of the bald man beside her and began to sob.

"What *is* to become of them?" Robert asked the Runner. Though his question lacked the passion of the sobbing woman, he was no less interested in the answer, for an idea had begun to form in his brain. "Have you any idea what they will do now?"

The Runner returned the silver toothpick to the corner of his mouth, as if the implement aided in his thought processes. "The way I see it, there's precious little they *can* do. They're in Queer Street, sir, and that's a fact, for if I know aught of the matter, actors seldom know 'ow to do anything but act."

"I see," Robert said as his idea grew, gradually shaping itself into a full-blown plan.

"It's 'ard luck, the theater owner locking up their scenery the way 'e did, for if they 'ad the props and such, most likely the troupe could finish up the tour without Ragsdale."

"Oh? Are they that resilient? Could they continue without a manager?"

"Wouldn't 'ave no alternative. Near as I can tell, Ragsdale owed every man jack of them for the entire month, and I'd bet my boots not one of them 'as enough money laid by to pay 'is shot at the inn. As for paying their passage back to London . . ." He let his voice trail off, as if there was no point in belaboring the obvious.

Robert glanced toward the inn yard again. Miss Townsend had joined another group, whose members greeted her with excited voices. While they all tried to speak at once, their concern for their immediate futures foremost in their stories, Robert returned his attention to Jethro Comstock. The Runner's face was a study in blandness, leading Robert to suspect there was more to be related. "Out with it, Comstock. Let me have the whole story."

"As it happens, sir, there is a mite more to tell. While the h'innkeeper was busy figuring up each man's shot, I 'appened to 'ear some of the town fathers, who were in the taproom 'olding a meeting. They were jawing amongst themselves, plotting 'ow they might toss the entire troupe onto a carter's wagon and dump them across the county line."

Robert said nothing, though he was not all that surprised by the scheme. He was not unacquainted with the practice of spiriting the indigent away and depositing them in another county. Villagers had enough to do to support their own poor without being required to extend charity to people who did not live in their parishes.

"H'its a bad situation all around."

The observation being indisputable, Robert ignored it. It was time to put his plan into action. "How much did Ragsdale owe?" he asked. "Have you any way of knowing?"

The Runner looked as though he might take offense at such a question. "I'm a detective, sir. H'it's my business to know."

"And?"

"H'in round figgers, sir, the bloke owed about two 'undred quid."

"Thank you," he said. Then, without another

word he strolled over to the group where Isobel Townsend stood. "May I speak with you?" he asked.

"I am sorry, Mr. Montford, but at the moment I have no time for—"

"It is important," he said. Then, remembering that he had used those words the evening before with little or no success, he amended the statement. "What I have to say is important to *you*. And," he added, lowering his voice so that only she could hear him, "perhaps to your fellow thespians."

Isobel wanted to tell him to mind his own business and be on his way, for he had already imposed his will upon her quite enough for one lifetime, but when he mentioned her fellow actors she could not refuse to listen to what he had to say. After all, he was a wealthy man, and when a person was destitute it behooved that person to listen to those who were in positions to offer assistance.

Swallowing her pride, she nodded, allowing him to put his hand beneath her elbow and lead her toward a large, wide-domed horse chestnut tree that stood in the far corner of the inn yard. Once they had reached the privacy of the tree, where dozens of shiny, reddish brown conkers had already fallen to the ground, she pulled her arm free. "I am listening, sir."

He ignored her rudeness. "I understand that the manager of your troupe has disappeared, leaving you and your friends without funds and, more importantly, without the means of earning your way back to London."

Not waiting for her confirmation of the story, he said, "I am prepared to offer whatever assistance is needed."

Isobel was not so naive that she mistook his words for a sign of impending Christian charity. "Your assistance," she repeated.

"Yes. I am willing to pay the debt owed to both the innkeeper and the theater owner, so your fellow actors may redeem the scenery and props and continue their tour."

"And in exchange for this unlooked-for kindness you will expect . . ." She paused, allowing him to complete the sentence for her.

"I will expect you to return with me to Montford House."

Somehow, Isobel had known that would be his answer. But, then, why should a man who had resorted to kidnapping yesterday cavil at a bit of blackmail today? "Sir, is there nothing you will not do to gain your own way?"

"I do only what I must, madam." Unrepentant, he added, "Will it be so bad? I overheard you say you were contracted to the Ragsdale troupe only through the end of July, and that after that time you were to portray Columbine at The Haymarket Theater in London."

"Yes, but—"

"I do not ask you to give up your engagement in London. To the contrary, I propose only that you spend the next two weeks as a guest in my home. At the end of the fortnight, I give you my word I will put you aboard a stage bound for Town."

He said nothing for several moments, giving her time to consider his offer. "Well? What say you, madam? Will you return with me to Montford House? Will you save your friends from destitution while giving untold joy to a woman whose health is still precarious?"

Isobel wanted to scream her frustration. How had she come to this—she who prided herself upon her independence? Orphaned at seventeen, she had been obliged to make her way in the world, and she had done so all on her own. She owed nothing to anyone—not Lady Baysworth, and certainly not this ragtag troupe of actors she had known for little more than a month. And yet, how could she live with herself if she knew she might have helped the members of the troupe and chose to do nothing? She knew the answer to that question—she could not allow more than a dozen people to become destitute when their rescue was within her power.

"Well?" he said. "I need your answer. What is it to be? Shall I pay the debts so the plays may resume, or shall I get into my coach and return to my home and the dear lady who is convinced you are the child of her long-lost sister?"

The words all but choking her, Isobel said, "Pay the debt."

His only response was a nod. "Pack your portmanteau, Miss Townsend, and have the porter bring it down to the coach. I will see to the necessary business and join you within the half hour."

"What of my costumes and my makeup? They are at the theater."

"Forget them," he said, already turning to leave. "Before you return to London, you may give me a bill for both your time and your theatrical rubbish."

Rubbish! Angry with herself for agreeing to go with him, and furious with him for blackmailing her into doing something she had no wish to do, Isobel picked up one of the conkers that lay on the ground beneath the tree and threw the flat-sided nut at his retreating back. To her surprise, the conker hit him on the nape of his neck. He stopped and reached back, his fingers searching out the spot where the missile had struck him, but he did not turn around.

Something about the way he hesitated, his face directed forward, told her that he knew what had hit him, that he knew as well who had thrown the unsophisticated object. When he continued toward the inn, Isobel smiled. She was glad she had hit him, and equally glad he knew she had done it.

"That will teach you," she called after him, "that I am not to be bullied."

Four

The next morning Isobel came awake slowly, stretching contentedly in the wide, feather bed with its pale pink counterpane. By actors' standards, it was early, not yet nine of the clock, but she had never been one to sleep late. Even when she remained at a theater until long after midnight, mending a costume or rehearsing a new part, she always rose long before the others of the troupe. An active person, she had far too much energy to loll about in bed when there were places to see and things to do.

A practical person, as well, she had decided sometime during the night that she would give up railing at the situation in which she found herself and try to make the most of the next two weeks. She would do what she could—while remaining truthful—to cheer Lady Baysworth; meanwhile, she would give herself permission to enjoy the unaccustomed luxury of Montford House and the beauty of the estate.

Isobel had been a young girl the last time she had had the time and the opportunity to be in the country. After she was sent to the female academy in Dover, she never returned to Kent. There was no point in it. Even before her father's death he had traveled constantly with his acting troupe, and the cottage in Ashbridge she had always thought of as home had been rented to another family.

It was the promise of a long walk about the grounds that prompted Isobel to throw back the covers and swing her feet to the floor. The deep, thick pile of the rose and green Axminster carpet tickled her bare toes as she padded across the room to the *chiffonnier*, where the maid had hung her clothes the day before.

At the recollection of the maid who had been assigned to see to her needs, Isobel shook her head. Aside from Mrs. Peabody, the village woman Thomas Townsend had hired to tend his infant daughter following the death of the child's mother, Isobel had little experience of servants.

Accustomed to looking after her own needs, she did not ring the bell that would summon the maid. Instead, she dressed herself, donning one of her half dozen frocks, a sprigged muslin with violet-colored inserts in the puffed sleeves. After buttoning her pair of sturdy walking boots, she brushed her long, thick hair and wound it into a knot, which she secured at the crown of her head. Eschewing headgear of any kind, she threw a Norwich shawl about her shoulders and hurried from the bedchamber.

"May I help you, miss?" asked a young housemaid who blushed profusely while bobbing an awkward curtsy. The servant had just emerged from the front saloon, a coal bucket and wiping cloth in her hands, so Isobel assumed she had been in there to clean out the grate.

"Thank you, but I think I know where I am going. I wish to see a small footbridge I spied from my bedchamber window. Is there a rear door I can use, or must I go out the front entrance?"

"There's the door leading to the kitchen garden, miss. If you'll follow me, I'll be pleased to show it to you."

Accepting the offer, Isobel allowed the young servant to lead her down a long, winding corridor to the rear of the house, hoping as she went that she would not require assistance in finding her way back. In a matter of minutes she was outside, breathing deeply of the invigorating morning air. The world seemed so fresh, so new, that Isobel longed to embrace it with her arms, to taste its clean coolness upon her tongue.

"And a proper fool you would appear if anyone saw you doing so," she muttered.

Putting aside such fanciful thoughts, she gave her attention to the neat, well-tended vegetable garden that lay to her right. At that hour of the morning the earth was still covered with dew, and the delicate beads of moisture turned all they touched into jewels. The dew that shimmered upon the cucumber vines transformed the bright green fruit into emeralds, and at the same time it sparkled upon the late-blooming rhubarb, causing the few remaining shards of the purple-red vegetable to resemble rubies fit for a sultan's crown.

Just beyond the garden was a narrow footpath worn smooth by generations of Montfords and their servants. Thinking of herself as the newest "smoother" of that rustic route, Isobel followed it for perhaps half a mile as it serpentined down a slight incline and then ended at a shallow, gently flowing brook. Because of the willow trees that grew down to the banks of the water, their velvety, blue-gray leaves often dipping low to the earth, she had not seen the brook from her bedchamber window, though she had guessed at its existence.

Patches of blue forget-me-nots dotted the area on the near side of the footbridge, while clumps of vivid yellow kingcup shone like gold all along the stream bank. Topping it all was the slightly arched bridge itself. Time had been kind to the structure, which was fully two hundred years old, turning the flint a majestic dark gray, while rich, pungent moss clung to the sides of the bridge as though stone and plant had come to an amiable agreement at least a century ago.

Isobel was enchanted by all she saw. For the next half hour she was content merely to stand upon the bridge, her elbows resting upon the parapet as she gazed down into the clear, clean water below and listened to the song of a sedge warbler. In defiance of her approach the little bird had emitted a rather shrill note of alarm—a surprisingly powerful note for so small a throat—but in time, when she offered no threat to the concealed nest, the little bird settled down, and its utterings modulated to a mellow, pleasant song.

It was the song of the warbler that covered the sound of Robert Montford's approach.

When Robert led Ajax, his handsome chestnut gelding, down to the water's edge for a cool drink, he had not expected to encounter his houseguest. Horse and man had traveled at breakneck speed across the open fields, for Robert was attempting to clear his mind of a most unpleasant scene between him and one of his tenants—Willem Potter, a man whose neighbor had accused him of stealing chickens from his poultry house. Robert had been inclined to believe the owner of the fowl, for this was not the first complaint against this particular tenant.

Furthermore, though Willem Potter attempted to ingratiate himself to his landlord by voicing a number of fawning compliments, he had the mean-eyed look of a man who blames all his misfortunes on other people. Not possessing the wisdom of Solomon, Robert had been unable to get to the bottom of the story, but he warned Potter that if there were another complaint—no matter how trivial—he would be obliged to terminate Potter's tenancy.

Later, after riding hard and fast, Robert had reined Ajax in at the brook to give the animal a breather. With the unpleasant confrontation with his tenant still in his thoughts, Robert had been unprepared to come upon Isobel Townsend. Spying her standing on the bridge, he stopped short. He must have muttered something, for she turned quickly, surprise writ plainly upon her face.

"Mr. Montford!"

"Miss Townsend. I had no notion you were here. Forgive me for startling you."

"No, no. Think nothing of it, sir."

He removed his tall-crowned hat and drew closer to the water, dropping the gelding's reins. "We always stop here," he said, as if needing to explain his sudden appearance. "I hope I have not trespassed upon your privacy."

"On the contrary," she replied, "I hope I have not trespassed upon a favorite spot of yours."

"Not at all, ma'am. That is to say, it *is* a favorite spot, but you are most welcome to partake of its beauty."

She smiled at him then. "Thank you. It is, indeed, quite beautiful."

Robert made no reply, for at her smile he was reminded that nature produced more than one sort of beauty. The young lady was dressed simply, with a shawl draped loosely across her shoulders, and because her head was bare, a soft breeze made free with her red-gold hair, causing several wispy curls to dance playfully about her temples.

While he gazed at her, a rather fanciful thought took hold of him—the notion that the pale blue of the sky had drifted down to blend with the dark blue forget-me-nots at his feet and that the two shades had merged, becoming one in Isobel Townsend's eyes. In danger of becoming lost in those lovely orbs, he forced his attention to her clear, smooth complexion. Her skin reminded him of peaches: pink and velvety and ripe for the picking.

Perhaps it was the thought of ripe peaches, or perhaps it was the fact that his gaze had strayed to her full, soft lips, but the word 'luscious' sprang to Robert's mind. As he studied her mouth, he found that his collar had grown uncomfortably snug.

He knew the cause; it was those kissable lips. They were having a marked effect on the temperature of his blood, and Robert suspected that if he did not think of something soon to deflect his thoughts, he would be obliged to push his horse aside so that he, too, could partake of the cooling influence of the water.

Giving voice to the first thing that entered his head, he said, "I must say, Miss Townsend, I am surprised to see you here at this hour. I had thought actors did not stir from their beds until the day was well advanced."

"Are you implying, sir, that I am a sleepwalker? I assure you, you see me quite awake."

She smiled to show that she was teasing, and as she trained those forget-me-not eyes upon him, Robert was reminded of the feeling that had taken hold of him while he had watched her portray Columbine two nights ago. Her hair had been loose at that time, the reddish blond tresses tumbling down her back, and her sweet, warm voice had filled his senses. For a few brief moments he had felt like one bewitched.

Now, here she was doing it again, with nothing but a smile!

While concentrating upon the gelding, who sipped daintily at the water's edge, Robert fought to regain control of his fanciful thoughts. "Madam," he said, hoping conversation would release him from the spell she had cast upon him, "I am bound for Montford House to break my fast. Have you found your appetite? Are you hungry?"

Pretending to misunderstand him, she waved a languid hand toward the willow trees, where the wind had disturbed the leaves, displaying their pure white undersides. Then, using a purposely overdramatic tone, she said, "How could I be hungry when I have partaken of the glories of these lovely surroundings? When I have ingested the song of the birds? When I have been nourished by the sound of the brook rippling over the rocky stream bed? When I have been—"

"Yes, yes," he said, not bothering to hide his smile, "but have you had any food?"

She chuckled. "Men! I vow they think of little else but their creature comforts. I begin to suspect, sir, that the members of your sex are all Philistines, every last one of you."

"I protest such censure, madam, for *I* am merely a pragmatist. And a hungry one at that." Gathering the horse's reins, he gave the animal a gentle tug to let him know it was time to go. "Ajax will be ready for his oats as well, so what say you, Miss Townsend? Shall we return to the house?"

Not waiting for her answer, he reached out his hand, and Isobel allowed him to assist her from the bridge. His fingers were strong and warm, the skin of his palm slightly rough, and at his touch Isobel felt an unexpected shiver of excitement race up her arm. Surprised at her own reaction, she reclaimed her hand the moment her feet touched the ground, then hurried toward the footpath, not once looking back to see if the gentleman followed.

"This has been a most delightful day," Agatha Montford said, setting her knife and fork across her plate and motioning for the butler to remove what remained of the fricassee of veal. "So delightful, in fact, that I almost wish it would not end. And we owe it all to you, my dear, dear Isobel, for Edith is much improved."

Isobel felt the heat of embarrassment in her face, and she was obliged to reach for the crystal wineglass beside her own gold-edged dinner plate. Because of her hostess's unwarranted praise of her, the veal that had tasted so delicious only moments ago seemed to turn to sawdust in her mouth. "I am happy that her ladyship is showing improvement, ma'am, but in all honesty I can take no credit for her renewed health."

"But of course you can. After your visit this morning, Edith ate a poached egg and half a currant bun, and this afternoon she drank an entire bowl of Cook's fortifying beef broth. Furthermore, she has promised to take tea with me later this evening." The lady lifted her napkin to the corner of her eyes and dabbed the moisture that had suddenly appeared. "I declare, I do not know what we would have done if you had not agreed to return to us. I am most grateful to you, my dear."

Unwilling to accept gratitude that was not rightfully hers, Isobel hurried to explain to her hostess just how she came to be at Montford House rather than in Norwich with the rest of the acting troupe. Unfortunately, the moment she mentioned Geofrey Ragsdale's name Robert Montford interrupted her, almost as if he wished the truth of their bargain to remain a secret between them.

"Speaking of actors, Mother, I do not recall your telling me how Fiona Cochran chanced to meet the actor with whom she eloped. Byron Smyth, I believe you called him?"

"That is correct."

Apparently not at all reticent to discuss an episode that had been the scandal of the neighborhood, his mother refused the raspberry trifle Kendrick offered her and began her story. "You were but four years old when Fiona left, so I cannot expect you to remember her, but you were quite fond of her. Everyone was, for she was full of fun."

She looked toward Isobel. "Fiona ran away twenty-five years ago last month. It was the thirtieth of June, and I remember it as though it were yesterday."

Interested in spite of her lack of connection with the runaway, Isobel said, "She must have been a rather daring young lady."

"She was an idiot," Robert corrected, "to commit such a reckless act."

"No, no, my boy. You are too harsh on her. Fiona was just young and headstrong, not to mention her having been spoiled from the cradle. Not that she could be blamed for that, of course. She was six years my and Edith's junior, and the child of middle-aged parents. What else could she be but petted and cosseted and given everything she ever wanted?"

"The chit could have been many things, Mother, but it appears she chose to be a fool. Albeit a beautiful one."

Mrs. Montford sighed. "My, yes. Fiona was as pretty as she could stare. All the young men were in love with her, and even a few who were no longer young cast eyes in her direction. She had not yet been up to Town, and Sir Harold had already refused three offers for her hand."

"You prove my point," Robert said, "for why would a young lady so much sought after—a chit whose birth and beauty would have assured her an advantageous marriage—want to ruin herself by running off with some itinerant actor?"

His mother shook her head. "That I cannot say. I imagine the answer lies somewhere between a girl's willfulness and a father's stubbornness. I am persuaded the entire episode would have come to naught if Fiona's parents had not forbidden her to so much as speak to the actor."

As if she recalled clearly her anger from long ago, the lady's face grew hard, pinching the corners of what was usually a gentle, rather pretty mouth. "They might have known how it would be, refusing the girl after seventeen years of indulging her every whim, but Sir Harold put his foot down, threatening to lock her in her room if she did not come to her senses."

Their guest obviously shared his mother's opinion of the matter, albeit a quarter century later, for she said, "And Fiona's father saw nothing incongruous in a parent who acts without reason, demanding reason of a spoiled child?"

Agatha Montford's answer was an unladylike *humph.* "Like many gentlemen, Sir Harold believed that once he had spoken the matter was settled. As you can imagine, such an order had the opposite effect from what he intended, for it turned Byron Smyth into forbidden fruit, making the actor appear even more appealing to Fiona. And you may believe me when I tell you that Smyth was already appealing enough!"

She sighed again, only this time the sound held an unmistakable hint of remembered infatuation. "Such a handsome man. Tall and blond as a Norse god. I should tell you he was that season's Hamlet, and the moment Fiona saw him she fell madly in love. Of course, we *all* did. I doubt there was a female for miles around who remained whole of heart."

"Et tu Brute?" Robert teased.

"Oh, yes," his mother admitted. "Though I saw Smyth for only that one performance, I must admit that when the fellow first appeared upon the stage my heart skipped a beat or two."

"Why, Mother!" Robert said, feigning shock. "And you a young wife with a small son."

Blushing, Agatha Montford adjusted the pretty lace cap that sat atop her soft brown hair. "I was but three and twenty myself—Miss Townsend's present age—and still young enough to be forgiven for admiring a handsome face and form."

"Of course you were," Isobel agreed. "Pray continue, ma'am. Was this Byron Smyth a competent actor?"

"Oh, more than competent. He had the most beautiful speaking voice, quite cultured, actually, and it became a popular game among the ladies to invent a background for him that would explain his refined manners and speech. If memory serves me, we finally decided he was the younger son of some duke or earl, and that he had been banished from his home and obliged to seek his fortune on the stage."

"A duke," Robert repeated. "What romantic nonsense. I am surprised you did not make him royalty and have done with it. After all, he was already playing the Prince of Denmark."

Not at all put out of patience by her son's lack of forbearance for a group of lovesick young females, Mrs. Montford said, "Byron Smyth *was* Hamlet, from the tips of his toes to the top of his blond locks, and those of us in the audience fairly hung on his every word.

"In fact," she continued, "I understand there was seldom an empty seat in the theater. I suppose I need not tell you that more often than not Fiona was among the assemblage. Naturally, I knew nothing of the secret trysts between Edith's sister and the actor, but at the end of the month, when the troupe and the blond Norse god packed up and moved south to Norwich, Fiona went with them."

"Was nothing done to recover the girl?" Isobel asked.

"Of course it was. Sir Harold led the search for his younger daughter, but after three weeks, when he had found no trace of the couple, he paid off the search party and returned to Gresham. Unfortunately, he had discovered no proof that a marriage had taken place between the actor and his daughter, so he disowned the foolish girl and forbade his wife and Edith to so much as mention Fiona's name in his presence."

Observing his mother's anger, even after all this time, Robert said, "Admittedly, Sir Harold's actions did not speak very highly of his supposed love for his child, but I doubt there are many fathers today who would welcome such a daughter back with open arms. Even if Fiona had married Smyth, actors are a disreputable lot. Surely no respectable person would rejoice to have one of them in his fami—"

At his mother's gasp, Robert realized what he had said. He looked quickly at their guest, who sat as though turned to stone, her gaze focused on the silver *epergne* in the center of the table. "Miss Townsend, I apologize. I did not mean—"

"Yes," she said, her voice devoid of emotion, "you did mean."

She said nothing more to him; instead, she returned her attention to his mother. "Pray continue with your story," she said, though the request sounded strained. "Did no one hear from Lady Baysworth's sister after her flight? Were there no letters, ma'am? No messages by word-of-mouth?"

Red-faced at her son's unthinking blunder, Agatha Montford hurried to cover the awkward moment. "There was not a word from her, my dear. It was as though Fiona Cochran and Byron Smyth had vanished from the face of the earth."

Five

Though Robert gave every appearance of listening to the remainder of his mother's story, he did not, in fact, hear a single word of it. He was too busy cursing himself for his gaucheness, his arrogance. Why had he not kept his mouth shut?

Actors are a disreputable lot, and no respectable person would rejoice to have one of them in his family. He could not believe he had said those words within Isobel's hearing.

His only excuse was that he had quite forgotten that she *was* an actor. Even so, she did not deserve to be tarred with such a broad stroke brush. Not only was she a pretty-behaved young woman, but for the entire two days that she had been in his home she had treated everyone—himself included—with a generosity of spirit that *he*, at least, did not deserve and had no reason to expect.

Were it not for her good nature, things might have been so different. Robert had practically forced her to come to Montford House—she had used the word "blackmail"—and yet she had chosen not to retaliate or to point a recriminating finger at him. Instead, she had been a surprisingly amiable guest, apparently having decided to make the best of a bad bargain.

As for her treatment of his godmother, nothing could have exceeded Isobel's gentleness. She spent hours in the sickroom, allowing Lady Baysworth to hold her hand and treat her as though she were, indeed, her niece, and the strategy was having a healing effect upon the invalid.

"And do you enjoy being on the stage?" he heard his mother ask.

Isobel had only just taken a sip of her wine, but she set the wineglass down and gave the question her full attention. "I do enjoy it," she replied, "at least for the most part."

His mother lifted a questioning eyebrow. "Not always?"

"No, ma'am. I enjoy performing," she said, the words spoken slowly, as though she had never voiced them before, "yet I find I have not the passion for it that drives most actors. If, for some reason, I should be obliged to leave the theater, it would not grieve me overmuch. Performing is something I know how to do, but it is not necessary to my happiness."

"And yet, my son informs me that you have a lovely singing voice."

Isobel made no reply, and after a moment she lifted her dessert fork and cut off a small portion of the trifle. "I work at my craft," she said, not raising the sweet to her mouth. "I strive constantly to learn and improve, and my diligence has paid off, for I have achieved a degree of proficiency that brings me a certain satisfaction." She smiled. "It also brings me ampler wages than would have been mine had I chosen some other career, a circumstance that enables me to remain independent."

"And is independence so important, my dear?"

"I believe it to be so, ma'am. If one is to—"

Whatever she had been about to reveal of her personal philosophy, it remained unsaid, for one of the footmen chose that moment to enter the dining room, a silver salver in his hand. Upon the small tray lay a white pasteboard visiting card, and after whispering something into the butler's ear, the servant surrendered both tray and card.

"Excuse me, madam," Kendrick said, bowing slightly, "but it seems there has been an accident in the lane just outside the entrance gates. Something involving a post chaise, I believe."

Agatha Montford gasped. "Was anyone injured?"

"I believe so, madam. As to the seriousness of the injuries, that I cannot report. Some assumption can be made, however, from the fact that the gentleman appears to have reached our door with only the assistance of his man. He waits just inside the vestibule, for he entreats the hospitality of the house."

She lifted the card and read the name aloud. "Cecil Wolcott." Apparently not recognizing the name, she glanced toward the head of the table, seeking her son's advice upon the matter.

"I will handle this," Robert said, rising from the table and walking toward the door. To the butler he said, "While I make the gentleman's acquaintance, Kendrick, be so good as to have a room prepared. And send word to the stable that one of the grooms might need to ride to the village for the apothecary."

"Yes, sir."

While the butler went to do his master's bidding, Robert strode down the corridor toward the vestibule. "Mr. Wolcott," he said, approaching the tall, rather distinguished-looking gentleman who leaned upon the arm of a manservant, "I am Robert Montford. I bid you good evening, sir, and welcome you to my home. I hope your injuries are not serious."

"More inconvenient than serious," replied the gentleman, his smile a fine blend of apology and self-mockery. "I would not trade upon your hospitality for the world, Mr. Montford, but I have only just come from London. Since darkness is descending, and I am unfamiliar with the neighborhood . . ." He let his voice trail off, as if the situation explained itself.

Robert offered no reply. He merely shook the gentleman's proffered hand, and as he did so he wondered which of the fates was toying with him by sending him two such disparate visitors: One a lady who would not tell a falsehood, and the other a gentleman whose first remark was a prevarication.

Only just come from London. It was a bold-faced lie, for Robert had seen Cecil Wolcott not two mornings ago in Gresham. The man had stood in the doorway of The Belled Cat, talking to the Bow Street Runner, and when he saw Robert, Wolcott had ducked out of sight.

"He's ever so handsome a gentleman, miss," the young housemaid said, "if I do say so as shouldn't, and a fine figure of a man, though he must be nigh on fifty. But I don't like his valet, not by half I don't. Mr. Zell, as he calls himself." She pointed her nose toward the ceiling, as if to imply the man gave himself airs. "He thinks himself quite above the rest of us, he does, and he's already set Mrs. Nidby's back up by asking for a breakfast tray instead of taking his mutton at the table, sociable like. You'd think he was valet to King George himself, the way he's so standoffish."

"Hmm," Isobel said.

She had been answering in monosyllables for the past ten minutes, for Isobel knew enough about servants to know it was bad form to gossip with them, especially about the members of the family. Unfortunately, Meg, the loquacious maid who had brought her a cup of chocolate, did not seem to take the hint that her chatter was falling upon unappreciative ears. The girl was full of news about the mysterious gentleman who had appeared out of nowhere last evening, and short of telling her to hush Isobel could not think how to stem the tide of the unwanted revelations.

"The gentleman's name is Wolcott," Meg said, "but with his valet being so uppity we've none of us discovered a thing about where they came from, or why they are in the neighborhood. Most likely the gentleman is on holiday," she added.

"Hmm."

"A pity about the wheel of his post chaise hitting a rock in the lane and tossing him out." Her sympathy obviously did not extend to the manservant, for she said, "Too bad it wasn't that snooty valet! Hurt his knee, the gentleman did, the right one, and he's in some pain—too much to leave his bed this morning, though he would not allow Mr. Montford to send for Mr. James. Poor gentleman."

"Hmm."

It was not at all clear to Isobel whether the "poor" gentleman was the man with the injured knee, the apothecary, or Robert Montford, but she did not seek enlightenment. Instead, she took refuge behind the cup of chocolate, raising the delicate china to her lips and swallowing. *Ugh!* One sip was sufficient, for the drink was thick as syrup, and cloyingly sweet! This was what a person got for lying in bed until nine of the clock—an undrinkable concoction served to her by a chattering magpie.

Isobel had chosen to remain in her room rather than go for the walk she truly wanted and risk another encounter with her host. Not that she had anything but pleasant memories of their meeting at the footbridge the day before. Unfortunately, those memories had been tarnished by Robert Montford's comments last evening about actors being disreputable.

There was some truth in his remark, of course, for Isobel had met a number of actors who deserved their ignoble reputations. Nonetheless, the barb had wounded her.

But worse was to come, for her host had continued, giving it as his opinion that no respectable person would wish to have an actor in his family. In that, at least, he was mistaken. After all, her father had been an actor, and Thomas Townsend was the best, kindest man she had ever known. As for her mother, Isobel felt certain that had Mary Townsend lived she would have been welcome wherever she went—even in the home of the judgmental Mr. Montford!

"According to Mrs. Nidby," Meg continued, bringing Isobel's thoughts back to the present, "it's a wonder lots more accidents don't happen in that lane. And she says it's a pure blessing the gentleman did not receive a more serious injury."

The maid reached for the unused brass candlesnuffer that lay on the bedside table and polished it with the tail of her apron. As she watched her, it occurred to Isobel that the girl was busying herself with unnecessary chores so she could remain to gossip.

After deciding there was but one way to rid herself of her informant, Isobel took a deep breath, raised the cup to her lips, tipped her head back, and drank every last drop of the unpalatable chocolate. "Thank you," she said, handing over the empty cup. "I have found my appetite at last, so I believe I will get up now and go down to the morning room."

"Shall I help you dress, miss?"

"No! That is, thank you, Meg, but I would prefer to do it myself."

Having committed herself to go belowstairs, Isobel donned a pale yellow muslin whose only adornment was a gold grosgrain ribbon that held the skirt in soft folds just beneath her bosom. When her *toilette* was finished and she could delay no longer, she made her way down the grand staircase and entered the cheerful pearl and azure room that faced the formal garden. Pleased to find the room empty, she was just serving herself a spoonful of basted eggs from one of the silver chafing dishes on the ebony sideboard, when Robert Montford entered the room.

As he had yesterday, he wore riding clothes, and his hair was slightly windblown, with one brown lock having fallen across his temple, giving him a carefree, relaxed look.

Unfortunately, Isobel was anything but relaxed.

With his arrival, she became so tense her hand shook as she replaced the serving spoon.

"You did not walk this morning," he said, the words almost an accusation. "Ajax and I looked for you at the bridge."

"I had no inclination to venture abroad this morning," she replied, her voice purposely cool.

If she had hoped he would accept her answer like a gentleman and not pursue the subject, she soon discovered the futility of such wishful thinking. "Was it because of what I said at dinner?"

Isobel felt herself blush, and the warmth made her angry. *She* had nothing for which to be embarrassed. It was the man before her who had offered insult, and she refused to allow him to rob her of her composure. "If you possessed the least pretensions to polite manners, sir, you would not remind me of remarks that are better left unrecalled."

"Ah, but there is the rub, madam, for I have no pretensions whatever to politeness. Far from it, in fact. Though, in all honesty, I wish I could have that brief moment back from last evening. If the time could be recaptured, I assure you I would unsay the words that offended you."

"And 'if wishes were horses, beggars might ride.' "

He lifted a questioning eyebrow, apparently not offended in the least by her less than forgiving rejoinder. "Shakespeare?"

"John Ray," she replied haughtily, turning her back to her host and pretending interest in the contents of the next chafing dish.

At that exact moment Agatha Montford entered the room, and they both turned to greet her. She looked like a breath of spring in a poppy-colored frock that complemented her slim figure and gave a touch of drama to her hazel eyes and the light brown hair arranged fashionably beneath her minuscule lace cap. Obviously having caught the last of their conversation, she forestalled their greetings by saying, "Did I hear someone mention horses? Are you taking Isobel riding, Robert?"

He glanced toward Isobel then, and the hint of victory in his dark eyes gave them a devilish glint. "I should be happy to take her riding, if she would enjoy the exercise."

"No, I thank you," Isobel said rather frostily. "I do not ride."

He stepped close to her, on the pretext of examining the breakfast choices. "You do not ride at all," he whispered, "or you choose not to ride with me?"

Isobel would have liked to tell him that she had no desire to be in his company, but she could not do so while his mother was within hearing distance. Instead she said, "I never learned to ride, sir."

"If she does not ride," his mother continued, apparently oblivious to Isobel's lack of enthusiasm, "you might take her for a drive in your phaeton."

"That is not necessary," Isobel said, moving away from the sideboard, "for I am quite content to remain here at—"

"I have it!" Her hostess smiled, the willing conduit of an inspired idea. "Robert can take you to The Broads. It is just the thing for a young lady of your adventurous nature, my dear, and I am persuaded that you will like the experience immensely."

"But, ma'am, I am not in the least adventurous, and I—"

"If you are worried about Robert, I pray you do

not, for my son always enjoys a day on the water. Do you not, my boy?"

"Ah, The Broads," repeated a deep, melodious voice from the doorway. "How I wish I might accompany you there, for I long to see those waters. It was to Horsey Mere that I was bound when ill fortune tossed me from my own *equipage.*"

All three inhabitants of the room turned to look at the tall, well-dressed gentleman who stood in the doorway, his hand resting upon the arm of a whey-faced servant—the unsociable Mr. Zell, Isobel presumed—but it was Robert who spoke first. "Mr. Wolcott," he said, bowing politely, "I had not expected to see you leave your bed today."

"No more, sir, than I had expected to do so. However, I cannot impose upon your good nature for more than one evening. Nor yours, dear lady."

This last was spoken to Agatha Montford, who appeared to have been sprinkled with pixie dust, for her mouth was slightly agape and her eyes were fastened upon the stranger. Not that Isobel blamed her, for the middle-aged gentleman was every bit as handsome as the chattering Meg had reported. His gray-streaked blond hair was combed back neatly from his clean-shaven face, and the simple hairstyle showed to advantage a classic profile—the kind of profile that is the envy of half the actors in England.

"Mother," Robert said, "may I introduce our guest, Mr. Wolcott? Sir, my mother, Mrs. Montford, and another guest, Miss Townsend."

The gentleman bowed again, first to his hostess and then to Isobel. "A pleasure, dear ladies."

"Sir," Agatha Montford replied, finding her voice at last, "it is a pleasure to meet you. I hope your injury did not rob you of your rest last evening. Sleep is a powerful healer, as I am sure you know."

"I believe it to be true, ma'am, and when I reach the next village, it is my plan to procure a room at the first inn I see. Once settled at the inn, I shall rest for the next several days."

"But, sir," his hostess hurried to say, "one never knows what one may find at the inns. They are quite undependable. Surely you would recuperate much faster if you remained here at Montford House."

The gentleman smiled, and Isobel fancied she heard Mrs. Montford sigh.

"You are too kind, dear lady, but I could not impose."

" 'Tis no imposition," the lady assured him. "None whatsoever." She turned to her son for the expected corroboration. "Tell him, Robert."

"None whatsoever," her son repeated, though to Isobel's ears his words lacked the sincerity of his mother's invitation. If Mr. Wolcott noticed the difference, however, he chose to ignore the fact, and soon he allowed himself to be convinced to remain a few days as their guest.

Within a short time the foursome were seated around the small, cloth-covered table. While Isobel had watched the injured gentleman being assisted across the room by his manservant, it had flitted through her mind that Meg had been inaccurate with at least one of her bits of gossip. Though the maid had reported that the fall had damaged Mr. Wolcott's right knee, the gentleman seemed to be favoring his left. Not that it was of the least importance.

"If we may return to the subject of The Broads," Robert Montford said, drawing Isobel's attention to him, "what say you, Miss Townsend? Shall we give them a try? I am completely at your disposal, for I have no pressing engagements this afternoon."

Isobel would have liked to fling the invitation back in his face, but the simple truth was that she had long wanted to visit one of the thirty or more lakes. Still, she hesitated, not certain she could be comfortable in her host's company.

"Come, come, madam," he teased, "you know you want to go. You must allow me to convince you, for this may be your one opportunity. After all, you might never come this way again."

At the remark, Mr. Wolcott shot him a startled glance, though the injured gentleman lowered his gaze almost immediately, giving his full attention to stirring a lump of sugar into his tea. After a moment or two, apparently satisfied with the blending of Bohea and sweetener, he set the spoon aside and returned his attention to his host, saying quite casually, "When you introduced Miss Townsend as a guest, I had no idea the young lady did not live in Norfolk."

"Miss Townsend is an actress," Robert replied, "and this is her first visit to Norfolk. She has, we are happy to say, agreed to stay with us until her next acting engagement, which is less than a fortnight away. For that reason, we must make what we can of the time she is at Montford House."

Isobel looked from one man to the other. Though she was not altogether pleased to be discussed as if she were not in the room, she kept silent upon the subject, for she had the oddest feeling there was an undercurrent of distrust between Robert Montford and his uninvited guest. At least, Robert seemed to harbor some sort of reservations about Mr. Wolcott.

As for the gentleman with the handsome profile, he appeared to have regained his poise and was now smiling at Mrs. Montford in a way that turned that lady's cheeks quite rosy.

"Well, madam," Robert said, reclaiming Isobel's attention, "have you made your decision? Would you like to see The Broads?"

"Yes," she replied, surprising herself with the answer, "I should like to. I will go with you."

Scarcely more than an hour later, still not certain why she had agreed to accompany him, Isobel sat beside Robert in a silver-trimmed, corbeau-colored phaeton pulled by a handsome pair of matched grays. To her relief her companion was a skillful driver, and as they traveled westward, passing through a small, neat village dotted with flint cottages overhung by reed-thatched roofs, she was able to relax and enjoy the feel of the fresh, warm air upon her skin.

Several people in the village paused to doff their hats or wave a friendly greeting at the passing carriage, and Isobel assumed these were mostly Montford tenants. She recalled a snippet of gossip Meg had related about one disgruntled tenant, but these people appeared contented enough.

Within minutes the high-stepping grays had left the village behind and turned onto a gently undulating forest trail. It was a serene, beautiful view, with majestic, broad-domed oaks growing in abundance on either side, and mingling with the occasional beech and maple were smooth-barked, wild cherry trees whose subtle, almond fragrance filled the air.

Little conversation had passed between driver and

passenger for the half-dozen miles the horses had already covered, but Isobel was doubtful that she could maintain the silence much longer. Even though Robert's thoughtless remark about actors had wounded her sensibilities, treating someone to a fit of the sullens was against Isobel's nature, especially when she was surrounded by so much beauty.

Hers was not the sort of temperament that brooded over past slights and supposed snubs, for it was a luxury she could not afford. She was engaged in a profession in which petty jealousies were a fact of life, and where undermining the worth of one's competition was an accepted practice. Over the past five years she had learned to turn a deaf ear to the little barbs sent her way by fellow artists, so why, she wondered, could she not do so now? Robert Montford meant nothing to her; why could she not simply forget his words, and get on with the job of living?

"As an actress," her companion said, surprising her out of her reverie, "I must suppose that you set dialogue to memory with little effort."

"Not at all, sir. Memorization comes no more easily to me than to any other person."

"Then how do you learn a new role?"

Considering his opinion of actors, Isobel had not expected the introduction of this particular topic. After stealing a glance at his serious profile, however, and finding nothing there to make her doubt the sincerity of his interest, she decided to answer his question. "I find it helpful in learning my lines if I picture the scene from beginning to end and listen carefully to the logical progression of the dialogue."

She was not certain that she was making herself understood, but she continued nonetheless. "If I put myself in the speaker's shoes, always keeping in the back of my mind the experiences and views that have shaped that character's beliefs, I find the lines of dialogue come naturally to me, allowing me to speak them with ease and, I hope, with integrity.''

"I see," he said. "And you always follow this procedure—this putting yourself in the character's shoes?"

"Always.''

She had no more than voiced her reply when he surprised her by reining in the horses, pulling them over to the side of the trail where they frightened a large brown hare into scurrying into the woods. Once the phaeton came to a complete stop, Robert reached inside his coat, withdrew a folded sheet of vellum, and offered it to her. "Would you be so kind as to read this?"

Though bewildered by his behavior, she took the paper, unfolded it, and began to peruse it silently.

"Aloud, if you please, Miss Townsend. Read it as though you were auditioning for the part."

She had already seen enough to be pretty certain what was written on the sheet, but she did as he asked and returned to the beginning.

"I once hoped to become a man of science," she read, slipping into the new role with ease of practice and speaking the words as though they were from her own experience. "I pursued that goal, knowing as I did so that as a man of science I must maintain an open mind, avoiding preconceived notions that would hamper me in my quest for scientific knowledge.

"While engaged in the systematic pursuit of truth," she continued to read, "I knew I must make no unfounded evaluations. My job would be to recognize a problem, then gather all available information upon the subject. I would observe. I would experiment. I would test the hypothesis. And lastly, I would draw as accurate a conclusion as was humanly possible."

Isobel paused, moistening her lips with the tip of her tongue, knowing where this speech was leading. "Sir, this is not necessary. I—"

"I promise you," he said, "the end is in sight. Do not stop just yet."

After taking a deep breath, she continued to read from the paper in her hand. "A man of science abhors the introduction of personal bias, for it does not evaluate the facts—it distorts them."

She paused again, lingering over the word *bias*. When she looked up from the vellum he said, "Please," and the softly spoken entreaty left her no recourse but to continue.

"Yesterday," she read, "I forgot the basic principles of science. I formed an opinion where there was no fact, only hearsay. A man of science does not give credence to unfounded rumor. He leaves such behavior to the fool. Yesterday *I* was that fool. Today I am ashamed of my behavior, and I ask your pardon."

Isobel spoke the final sentence. Then she refolded the paper, trying not to let him see how much her hands shook. He had no idea what it was like for an actor to assume the *persona* of another individual, how very personal the experience could be. If the truth be told, speaking his words had been more revealing than even Isobel had expected. For a few moments she had looked into Robert Montford's soul, experienced his longing to return to the science he loved, and the insight had left her more in sympathy with him than she could have imagined.

"You are forgiven," she said quietly, handing the paper back to him. "I should have allowed you to apologize this morning when you first entered the breakfast room, and for that refusal I beg *your* pardon. It is not like me to act so churlish, and with your permission I propose we let what is bygone remain bygone."

"An excellent suggestion," Robert said. Impressed by her generosity in allowing him to make amends, he offered her his hand. "Friends?"

"Friends," she repeated. Then, after only a moment's hesitation, she laid her hand in his. To Robert's surprise, when she touched him he felt an almost overwhelming desire to draw her close, to wrap her in his arms and beg her forgiveness with a kiss.

Luckily, before he could act on that thought and ruin the newly achieved peace between them, she eased her hand from his. "As an actress," she said, giving him a rather saucy look, "there is one thing more I must know."

Robert was not immune to the smile that lit her eyes and pulled at the corners of her mouth, and it was all he could do to wrest his gaze from those full, tantalizing lips. "Ask what you will of me," he said, answering her smile with one of his own. "What is it you wish to know?"

"Only this," she replied. "How was my reading? Did I get the part?"

Six

The beauty of The Broads exceeded its reputation, and to Isobel the small portion of it she saw was the closest thing on earth to the Garden of Eden. In excess of thirty lakes were joined with local rivers and some interconnecting waterways to form a sort of triangular area that stretched from Lowestoft to Norwich and to Sea Palling and back. Though she had heard much of the exotic birds and the profusion of wildflowers, not to mention the peaceful waters, she had not guessed at the vastness of the phenomenon.

"This is breathtaking," she said, her words hushed as if in homage to the unspoiled spectacle stretched out before her.

She had cupped her hands around her eyes to shade them from the glare of the sun on the water and was gazing across the shallow lake to the opposite shore, where a gentleman had rowed his boat partway through a nearly impenetrable reed jungle. His object, obviously, was to impress the young lady he escorted by attempting to catch one of the dozens of gold and black swallowtail butterflies that hovered above a clump of bright pink marsh orchids.

He did not succeed in capturing the butterfly, but

very nearly capsized the boat in his frenzied attempt, and his fair companion began to scream as though she were already drowning. At her screeching, at least a dozen frightened waterfowl took flight, protesting loudly at this forced abandonment of their food gathering.

"I wish their boat had tipped over," Isobel muttered.

"Tsk, tsk, Miss Townsend. A most unsportsmanlike sentiment."

"Fair is fair," she countered.

"Would you have the lady and gentleman fall into the water and ruin their clothing?"

"Had they caught the butterfly, it would have been nothing more than justice. After all, what right have they to steal from nature's creation?"

"Actually, you may credit nature with improving the place, but you must not credit her with its creation. There is much evidence to prove that the lakes were the work of medieval man."

Isobel dropped her shielding hands and turned to stare at him. "Are you making a May game of me, Mr. Montford? Surely The Broads predate history. As for medieval man, how could he have created this beauty? I claim no great knowledge of that period, but according to all I have ever read the lives of those people were pretty cheerless, consisting of little but toil and more toil. When were they supposed to have had time to recreate Paradise?"

"I shall be happy to answer your question," he said affably, "but first you must agree to pay the price."

While he spoke he put his hand beneath her elbow and began leading her across the springy ground, its mossy green surface dappled by the sunshine that filtered through the trees.

"What price, sir? And where are you taking me?" she asked, eyeing a small boat dock up ahead, where an enterprising local man sat guarding a half-dozen brightly painted punts.

"Patience," her escort said, continuing toward the boats.

A sign affixed to one of the dock pilings read: *Boat Rental One Shilling The Day;* and after reading the sign, Isobel freed her elbow from Robert Montford's grasp. "If the price of your answer is a shilling, sir, be advised that I have not the least intention of riding in one of those leaky old boats, and I certainly would not *pay* for the privilege."

"Never tell me you are *afraid,* Miss Townsend."

"Afraid? I will say only that the fish and I have a bargain. As long as they do not venture onto the land, I do not invade their territory."

His chuckle seemed to echo off the water. "Your bargain with the fish notwithstanding, ma'am, riding in one of those punts was not the payment I had in mind."

"Of *course* it was not," she said, her suspicious tone giving the lie to her words.

He laughed again. "I meant merely to ask you, since we are to be friends, if you would do me the honor of calling me by my name."

It was a simple request, and one that any gentleman might ask, yet somehow the idea of such familiarity between them caused a momentary flutter in Isobel's midsection. Here was missishness indeed! The man had not asked her to marry him. He had simply asked her to call him by his name.

After admonishing herself for making more of the request than it merited, she placed a purposely false smile upon her face. "I should be happy to call you by your name, *Robert,* sir, but it will change nothing. I *still* refuse to set foot in that boat."

"Coward," he said. "I had thought you made of sterner stuff. After all, you stand upon the stage night after night and perform before hundreds of strangers, a situation guaranteed to give even the strongest person a case of quaking knees."

"I assure you, sir, I suffer from no such malady, for I can *walk* on the stage. Unfortunately, I possess no such ability on the water."

As it transpired, he would not allow her to cry craven, and before Isobel knew what he was about she found herself being assisted into one of those punts. After clutching his hands with enough force to inflict permanent damage upon less powerful fingers, she was soon seated in the pointed end of the narrow, flat-bottomed boat, with Robert standing in the square end, propelling them by use of a long pole.

Fortunately for Isobel's peace of mind, the gentleman gondolier appeared to know what he was doing, and in a matter of minutes she relaxed, loosening her death grip upon the sides of the wooden boat and giving herself up to the pleasure of gliding slowly across the water. Her fear dispelled, she began to feel at one with nature, not unlike the great crested grebe who swam past the boat, his long white neck raised high above the water, and his bright red ear tufts spread wide as if to capture the warmth of the sun.

The lady and gentleman traversed the peaceful

lake in companionable silence for a time, passing myriad birds and two other punts. Then finally Isobel said, "Well, sir, what say you? I have paid the price, and you see me sitting here docile as any lamb, yet you continue to keep to yourself the answer to my question as to what medieval man had to do with The Broads. How came he to create this beautiful spot?"

Though Robert continued to pole the punt in a smooth, effortless manner, he looked at her, mock innocence on his face. "You misunderstood me, for I said nothing about medieval man creating this beauty. I merely mentioned that the lakes were his doing."

"Sir, you are sorely trying my patience. If you do not give me that information for which I have paid, I shall be obliged to call to the owner of the boats, advising him that I have been lured onto the water with false promises. After that, let it be on your head if he fetches the local authorities."

"Madam," Robert said, his tone studiedly bland, "does the word 'blackmail' mean anything to you?"

"Of course it does," she replied, batting her eyelashes as if she were the personification of innocence. "I learned the word a few days ago, when a certain gentleman—a recent acquaintance, I might add—saw nothing wrong in using that very method against me to achieve his goals."

"Ah, yes," Robert said, not the least discomfited, "I thought it seemed familiar."

A gurgle of laughter escaped Isobel's throat, but she quickly smothered it. *"Medieval man?"* she prompted.

"As you wish."

After lifting the pole from the water and laying it across the boat, Robert moved slowly, cautiously, and sat down, his booted feet touching hers in the small space.

"There is evidence," he began, "that at one time—perhaps as long ago as three or four thousand years—this entire area was nothing but thick, exposed layers of peat."

"Peat? Here?"

"Exactly. It is a known fact that during the eleventh and twelfth centuries, perhaps even earlier, the peasant classes supported themselves by digging up the abundant fuel and selling it in Norwich, which was already a thriving town. The best and most widely accepted hypothesis is that more than two thousand acres of peat may have been excavated during those two centuries."

"My word. They were an industrious lot, those medieval peasants."

"To be sure," he replied. "As you can imagine, digging out that much peat—though it was probably less than a tenth of the entire deposit—left sizable holes in the landscape."

"Sizable? I should think that an understatement, sir. But how did the land go from, er, *decimated* peat bogs to these beautiful lakes?"

Robert smiled in appreciation of her pun, but he did not comment, choosing instead to continue with his story. "It is believed that at some time during the thirteenth century there was a gradual rise in sea level, a rise that resulted in a steady flooding of the old peat-digging areas. Though the sea waters receded somewhat toward the end of that century, the land did not drain completely, and over time a mingling of sea and river water formed the basis for the many lakes. As for the beautification, nature required the next five hundred years to complete that task, leaving The Broads as you see them today."

Isobel found the hypothesis fascinating. "And is there proof of this, or is it merely a theory?"

"There is proof," he replied, "though it is inconclusive at the moment. However, those men who have embraced the study of paleo-science are unearthing more evidence every year."

From the wistfulness in the gentleman's voice, Isobel had little doubt that Robert Montford yearned to be one of those embracers of paleo-science, one of those men who were actively *unearthing* information and proving theories. "And where do these learned men seek their proof?"

"Down there," he replied, indicating the area beneath the lake. The reflection of his hand and pointing finger moved in and out of focus with the gentle movement of the brackish water. "The proof needs only to be dug up."

Robert could not remember the last time he had experienced such an enjoyable day, or been in the company of such a delightful companion. It did not take him long to realize that Isobel Townsend was more than just another pretty woman. She possessed a quick, inquisitive mind and, added to that quality, she was courageous, for it had taken real pluck for her to put aside her fear of the water and climb into the punt. After accepting his word that no harm would come to her, she had set herself to enjoying the outing, displaying none of the missish behavior one might expect from a female with no experience of boating—one who, by her own admission, could not walk upon water.

A woman in one of the other punts had squealed every time a small wave caused the boat to rock, and once she had burst into tears when her inept swain, unable to control the oars, had splashed water in her face and liberally doused her skirts. Isobel treated Robert to no such histrionics, though she had quietly gripped the sides of the boat on one or two occasions.

Even when a passing grebe uttered a loud *cuck, cuck, cuck* of disapproval at their invasion of his private domain, the young lady did not flinch. Later, when they returned to the dock and Robert helped her out, holding her by the shoulders until she regained her land legs, she had looked up at him and smiled. "Thank you," she had said, her words slightly breathless, "for a marvelous adventure."

Robert had stood as if transfixed, enjoying the feel of her soft flesh beneath his fingers. While he gazed into her upturned face, his attention riveted on the pert nose that was slightly pink from the sun, he had decided she was the prettiest girl he had ever seen. "You are welcome," he had said.

During the return journey to Montford House, Robert regaled her with tales of some of his youthful explorations of the Norfolk area. "I was forever digging about for likely fossils," he said. "My mother could never keep me at home, and when I did return I was invariably covered in dirt."

Isobel chuckled. "If you were anything like the young boys I knew in Kent, I suspect you came home disgustingly grubby."

"Oh, decidedly grubby," he admitted, laughing as

she had done. "I was never allowed through the front door, for I would be filthy from head to foot, and my pockets would be bulging with fossilized insects and fragments of bones I was convinced were those of dinosaurs."

"Bones? Insects?" Isobel shuddered. "Poor Mrs. Montford. You said she could never keep you at home. With such loathsome 'finds' in your pockets, it is a testament to a mother's love that she did not deny you the house!"

He feigned insult. "And I suppose you were a pattern of ladylike behavior."

"But of course. One hates to brag, sir, but the simple truth is that I was perfect in every way. A model of little girl deportment."

He lifted an eyebrow in disbelief. "You sound an absolute paragon."

"The very word," she said. "If the truth be known, sugar and spice do not even *begin* to paint the proper picture."

"That," he said, his voice dripping with sarcasm, "I can readily believe."

They had left the forest trail and were passing through the village when she asked him if he were able to put a name to any of the fossilized insects he had discovered.

"Many of them," he replied. "My mother gave me an excellent book on geology that contained numerous drawings of the prehistoric flora and fauna of England, and I labeled every insect I could recognize."

"If you have the fossils still, I should like to see them."

Suddenly suspicious, Robert gave her a sidelong

glance to see if she spoke the truth. As the wealthiest man in the neighborhood, he was not unaccustomed to being pursued by marriageable females, and he had not lived twenty-nine years without discovering a few things about the members of the opposite sex. Marriage was their primary goal, and in pursuit of an eligible man young ladies were not above pretending interest in the gentleman's pursuits simply to attract his attention.

If Isobel Townsend was among that number, however, he saw no indication of it. Though she was inquisitive, he knew enough of her to recognize that feature as part of her personality, and when she looked at him her countenance was open and honest, showing no signs of duplicity.

Satisfied that she was truly interested, he said, "Perhaps you would prefer to unearth a specimen or two yourself. I could take you to Cromer Ridge. It lies but a few miles to the east of us, so it is not too far removed for a day's outing."

At the issuance of the invitation, she searched his face as he had searched hers only moments earlier, as if she, too, suspected some hidden purpose. "Forgive my hesitation, sir, but I have learned to be somewhat guarded when it comes to your suggested outings. Pray, enlighten me. If I consent to accompany you to this place, will I be required to risk my very life in an even more disreputable boat?"

He shook his head. "This time, Miss Townsend, you may remain on the land."

"You promise?"

"Word of a gentleman."

"In that case, sir, I should be happy to—"

"Of course," he continued, unable to resist teasing her, "there is just the least little insignificant amount of mountain climbing involved."

"Mountain climbing!"

"Yes, but I am persuaded you will not mind that."

She gave him a very telling look. "You believe that, do you?"

"Why, yes, for I am confident that a lady of your spirit would find the experience quite exhilarating. Is tomorrow too soon?"

"If the excursion involves an activity as dangerous as mountain climbing, then next *year* is too soon. And while I am on the subject, sir, allow me to disabuse you of the completely unfounded notion that I would fall in with such a scheme."

He acted surprised. "But why would you not?"

"Why? Because I have no more desire to pitch headlong over the side of a mountain than I have to be tossed into a lake. You may find this difficult to believe, sir, but I am even less adept at flying than I am at walking on water. And, lest you think that just because I gave in today at The Broads, I will do so again, let me tell you that you are mistaken."

"If you go," he said, ignoring her argument, "I can show you something quite fascinating. I promise you, it is something you will not forget as long as you live."

Robert could tell from the spark of interest in her eyes that she was tempted. "It is older than man," he continued, his tone not unlike that of a rider offering a lump of sugar to a shy horse. "Older even than most of the animals that now roam the earth."

Her sigh was one of resignation. "I surrender. What is it you wish to show me?"

The horses had already passed through the brick

columns that supported the entrance gates, and now their hooves sounded on the crushed rock carriageway. In the distance, the late afternoon sunset turned the Palladian-style house a mellow pink. As the grays neared the ivy-covered walls of the house, Robert thought he had never seen his home look more dignified.

Or more deserted!

Where was everyone? And why had none of the stable lads come to take charge of the horses?

"What is it?" Isobel repeated, though Robert was not misled into thinking she still spoke of the promised outing. "Is something amiss?"

Isobel had sensed the sudden tension in the man beside her, but—unfamiliar with the practices of the estate—she could not even guess at what had put that concerned look on his face. "Has something happened?"

"Perhaps," he replied, "but speculation is pointless at the moment. I imagine we shall discover all as soon as Kendrick opens the door."

As it happened, Kendrick did not open the heavy front door. The ever-efficient butler was nowhere to be seen, and the master of the house was obliged to let himself into the vestibule. "Hello," Robert called. "Where is everyone?"

"Here, sir," came a timid reply.

The voice was female, and it came from the rear of the corridor that led to the kitchen. The response was followed by the sound of running feet, and within a matter of seconds Meg appeared. The young housemaid was breathless, and her face was flushed. As well, her once-starched apron was soiled, her mobcap was askew, and if red eyes were anything to go by she had only recently given in to a bout of crying.

"Oh, sir," she said, bobbing a hasty curtsy, "thank heaven you have come."

"What is it, girl? Has something happened to Lady Baysworth?"

"No, sir. Her ladyship and me are just about the only ones not taken to our beds with the bellyache. The entire household—every last servant, from Mr. Kendrick down to the stable lads, not to mention Mrs. Montford—is sick. Folks been falling like apples off a tree, they have, since early afternoon. And now they've started casting up their accounts. I've near run my legs off trying to do for everyone, and there's not a clean pot left in the house."

Having said her piece, the rattled servant covered her face with her apron and began to sob as though her heart would break.

Leaving the weeping maid to Isobel, Robert took the steps two at a time, not stopping his quick pace until he reached his mother's bedchamber. To his relief, she was not too weak to bid him come in, though she lay upon her bed, the window hangings drawn to reduce the light in the room, and a damp cloth covering her eyes. After ascertaining that she was in no real danger, he commiserated with her regarding her discomfort. Then he asked if she could recall when the malady first made itself known.

"Shortly after the midafternoon tea," she replied. "I thought it quite nice at the time—the tea, I mean—for Cook had baked some of her delicious ratafia cakes and prepared a dish of strawberries picked from the garden only minutes before. There was clotted cream, of course, to pour over the berries, but it tasted fresh and sweet."

"The menu sounds innocent enough. Was there anything more, or was that all?"

"That was all, with the exception of the little beef tartlets with the béchamel sauce. But the tartlets could not be the culprit, for I had only one of those, even though they were especially savory, filled as they were with onions and grilled mushrooms. Still, I had to choose between a second serving of strawberries and another tartlet, and the berries won. It is probably my own fault, my boy, for you know how fond I am of strawberries. I am a grown woman, and I ought to have been content with the one serving."

He did not agree with her evaluation, but he kept that fact to himself. "Who took tea with you?"

"Why, Edith, of course. Kendrick brought the tray up to Edith's bedchamber. Oh, and our guest, Mr. Wolcott, joined us."

"Oh?" Robert said, suddenly alert. "How did a virtual stranger come to share an intimate meal between friends?"

"I invited him." His mother's cheeks, which had appeared ashen beneath the wet cloth, now turned a decided shade of pink. "I thought Edith might enjoy seeing a new face. And . . . and I was correct, for we had such a nice time. Mr. Wolcott is a most interesting gentleman. He could not have been more entertaining."

Robert did not doubt that for a minute, but whatever his thoughts about their guest, he chose to remain quiet upon the subject.

Unaware of her son's misgivings about the injured gentleman, Mrs. Montford continued. "Cecil—Mr.

Wolcott, I should say, though he asked Edith and me to call him by his name—told us about Wolcott Park, his home in Sussex. Actually, it is his brother's home, for his brother is the fifth Baron Wolcott, but when Cecil became a widower several years ago he returned to the family home to run the estate for Lord Wolcott."

Storing for later use the information about their guest's occupation and his place of residence, Robert asked his mother about Lady Baysworth. "Since my godmother suffered no ill effects from the tea, I am curious to know if, like you, she tasted some of everything served."

"No, Edith wanted only tea and toast, and since she is showing such improvement these past few days, I made no fuss about her eating more."

"So she sampled none of the ratafia cakes or the strawberries? What of the beef tartlets?"

His mother shook her head. "Just the tea and toast. What is this about, Robert? From your questions, not to mention the serious look upon your face, one might be forgiven for thinking you suspect Mrs. Nidby of poisoning us."

"Cook? Not at all, Mother. The thought never entered my mind."

As if only just thinking of it, he asked quite casually, "By the way, should I go see our most recent houseguest, do you think—just to assure myself that he, too, did not fall victim to this unfortunate malady?" Before his mother could reply, he added, "Did Mr. Wolcott find it difficult to choose between the strawberries and cream and the beef tartlet? Or did the gentleman perhaps refuse one of the selections entirely?"

His mother sighed, as though she had endured enough discussion of food for one day—especially *this* day. "I believe he allowed Kendrick to serve him a little of everything."

"So, he ate the tartlet?"

"Robert! I cannot think of anything more apt to make a guest feel *de trop* than his hostess taking notice of what he does or does not eat. Besides, I feel certain he tried the—No. Wait. Now I think of it, I do not believe he even tasted the tartlet. Not that there is anything remarkable about a guest not eating everything he is served. After all, personal preferences vary. In this instance, Cecil might not care for béchamel sauce."

"As you say, ma'am. Such an aversion would, of course, explain the gentleman's reticence."

Later, when Robert went belowstairs to the kitchen to question the housemaid about the number of staff who had eaten the beef tartlets, he found Isobel Townsend there. To his surprise, she had donned a white apron so large it needed to be wrapped twice around her trim waist, and now she stood beside the cavernous fireplace, stirring the contents of a black caldron that bubbled noisily. The fragrance of barley soup filled the air, and when Isobel turned at the sound of his entrance, he noticed that the heat of the fire had caused her face to glisten with moisture, and that tiny, reddish-blond curls had sprung up around her temples.

Momentarily forgetting the purpose for which he had come to the kitchen, he said, "Madam, what in blazes are you doing?"

"Being useful," she replied affably. "The house is filled to overflowing with sick people, and very soon some or all of them will be in need of sustenance. If I know anything of the matter, a nice barley soup is just what will be wanted."

"But, but—"

"If you are offended that I stepped in to be of assistance, let me assure you I have no designs upon the cook's position. Besides, much more competent help should be arriving within the hour, for I sent Mr. Zell to the village to fetch the apothecary and to see if he could bring back some temporary kitchen help."

Quite certain he owed Isobel a debt of gratitude—yet unsure what he ought to say in the face of her no-nonsense practicality—Robert ignored for the moment the subject of her culinary services. Instead, he latched on to the one thing she had mentioned that caused him no embarrassment. "Who the blazes is Mr. Zell?"

The young housemaid dropped a curtsy. "If you please, sir, Mr. Zell is Mr. Wolcott's valet."

"Oh, is he? Then I presume he does not number among those so recently indisposed."

"Oh, no, sir," Meg replied. "Else he could not have ridden to the village."

"An astute observation," Robert said, and though the words were spoken rhetorically Meg blushed profusely.

"Th-thank you, sir."

Apparently unaware of the maid's embarrassment at being so long in the presence of her employer, he said, "How fortuitous that both servant and master managed to remain healthy when all about them people were—as you so aptly put it—falling like apples from a tree."

Though this remark was meant for Meg, it was Isobel who replied. "Mr. Wolcott's valet is not sociable, and he chooses to take his meals apart from the household servants."

"Ah," Robert replied, "then it would appear that the man's standoffishness has been its own reward. One must assume that he, like his master and Lady Baysworth, did not partake of the beef tartlets. And speaking of the tartlets, do you know, Meg, if Cook had the ingredients from the village?"

"All save the mushrooms, sir. They were a gift."

"A gift? From whom?"

Meg shook her head. "No one knows, sir. I was here when Mrs. Nidby discovered them, a nice new basketful just waiting outside the kitchen door. And quite a surprise they were, all neatly brushed, with the stems trimmed close to the caps, and covered over with a clean cloth. What with the new basket and the clean cloth, Mrs. Nidby allowed as how the mushrooms must be a gift from the wife of some grateful tenant."

Feeling Isobel's eyes upon him, Robert forestalled her questions by thanking the maid for the information and sending her to the larder to see if any of the tartlets remained. "If there are any, under no circumstances are you to taste them. Instead, bring them directly to me. And if you see the basket that contained the mushrooms, bring that as well."

Once Meg was out of hearing, Isobel moved away from the bubbling cauldron, stepping close to Robert. "What is it? What do you suspect?"

He did not hesitate to take her into his confidence, for he felt implicitly that she could be trusted. "I suspect that the mushrooms were poisonous."

"No! What a dreadful accident."

"If it *was* an accident."

He had kept his voice low so they would not be overheard, and when she answered him she spoke softly, as well. "Surely you cannot believe it was anything but an honest mistake."

"I can, and I do."

"But who would commit such a vile deed? I know little of mushrooms, but I understand that some varieties can be deadly."

When he vouchsafed no further comment, she said, "I pray you are mistaken, Robert, but if you are not, then whoever left that basket is a villain." As if saying the word made her flesh crawl, she shuddered. "Who could have purposely inflicted pain on an entire household? And why would he commit such a dastardly act?"

"I do not know the answer to either question," Robert replied. "But I promise you, I mean to find out."

Seven

The following morning all but two of the servants were able to leave their beds and resume their duties, though they did so with rather sallow complexions and fervent requests to remain as far away from the aromas of the kitchen as was possible. For Robert and his mother, the unpleasantness of the previous day was all but forgotten in their joy at the unexpected appearance belowstairs of Lady Baysworth, who joined them at about midday in the small, informal drawing room at the front of the house.

Because her ladyship's arrival was greeted with such sincere enthusiasm by the three inhabitants of the room—with her childhood friend rushing to enfold her in a tearful hug and her godson bestowing a gallant kiss upon her hand before ushering her to a comfortable chair—only Isobel noticed the entrance of Mr. Cecil Wolcott several moments later. Recuperations seemed to be the order of the day, for the gentleman had eschewed the sustaining arm of his valet, choosing instead to make his way unaided.

As Isobel watched him enter the room, she marveled that even though he was obliged to limp he lost none of his air of assurance. Dressed in tan breeches and a beautifully tailored blue coat that suited his gray eyes and his graying blond hair, he was most distinguished looking, the kind of man who generally commanded the attention of all those within his view.

Since the Montfords were occupied in making Lady Baysworth comfortable, Isobel smiled a welcome to the injured man and crossed the room to offer him her arm. He accepted her assistance, of course—he could not have done otherwise—but he bid her no verbal greeting, only a polite if somewhat cool bow of his head.

Isobel pretended not to notice behavior that bordered on a snub, but she could not help wondering what she had done to merit such treatment from one who was practically a stranger. Moments later, her puzzlement became even more pronounced, for while they progressed slowly toward a red damask settee, Mr. Wolcott limping the entire way, Isobel observed a most peculiar fact—the gentleman was favoring the wrong leg! Unlike yesterday, when he took special pains to protect his left knee, today he appeared to be protecting his right one.

Shaken by this discovery, Isobel kept her gaze trained on the settee, not wanting to look the man in the eyes lest he see that she had taken note of the physiological phenomenon of injury transferral.

Of course, shifts in point of impairment were not all that uncommon to her, for she was an actress, and those little inaccuracies often occurred on the stage. False injuries lacked the pointed reminder of pain. However, a careless actor could depend upon a helpful fellow thespian to whisper in an aside that the patch was over the wrong eye or that the *other* arm should be cradled in the sling.

Mistakes of that nature were just a part of the theater, and they were usually laughed off, with no more serious result than a bit of embarrassment for the offending actor. But this was not the theater, and Mr. Wolcott's mistake could not be attributed to an understudy's lack of preparation or the need for a quick costume change.

The man was practicing a deception. His so-called injury was a lie, and whatever his reasons for dissembling, Isobel knew she could not let his duplicity go unreported, especially not after yesterday's episode with the mushrooms. She must tell Robert what she had discovered.

With that object in mind, she searched her brain for a way to have a private moment with her host. As it happened the opportunity presented itself only a few moments later, when Lady Baysworth announced that she meant to dine with the family that evening.

"How marvelous," Mrs. Montford exclaimed. "We shall make it a real celebration. What say you, Robert? Shall we have Kendrick decant the last of the French brandy so we may drink a toast to Edith's health?"

"Consider it done," her son replied.

Here was Isobel's opportunity. "With your permission, ma'am," she said, "I should like to help. May I cut some roses from the garden to arrange in the *epergne?*"

Both ladies turned indulgent smiles upon her, making Isobel feel uncomfortably like a liar herself.

"You may gather whatever you wish, my dear. It

cannot fail to lift Edith's spirits to have flowers arranged by you."

"Indeed," her ladyship replied, a look of adoration in her eyes. "My mother had a gift for flower arranging, as did *your* mother. And I am persuaded that anything you choose to do will be similarly lovely."

At her ladyship's remark, the gentleman beside Isobel had stiffened, but now he turned to look at her, a practiced smile upon his face—a smile that did not quite reach his eyes. "I must say, Miss Townsend, you are not unlike the rose yourself, with pretty petals protecting the real flower beneath. Each time we meet another petal is removed, and I discover some hitherto unsuspected fact about you. Can it be that you are related to Lady Baysworth?"

"No, sir, I—"

"Yes," her ladyship replied at the same instant. "The young lady is my niece."

"Ma'am," Isobel corrected, "I have explained to you that I cannot possibly—"

"Now, my dear," Agatha Montford interrupted, casting a pleading look toward Isobel, "let us not spoil this lovely afternoon with references to the past."

"But, ma'am, I—"

"Robert!" his mother interjected. "Perhaps you would be so good as to escort dear Isobel to the garden? Show her the China roses. The Bouquet d'Or should do nicely for the *epergne*. Such a lovely fragrance."

Robert Montford stood, making an abbreviated bow in Isobel's direction. "I am yours to command, Miss Townsend. Shall we go now?"

Since it was her wish to speak with Robert, Isobel did not delay but stood as well, curtsying to the ladies. "Excuse me," she said.

"Of course, my dear."

Isobel walked slowly, as if she had nothing more important than flowers on her mind, but the moment she and Robert were in the corridor, the drawing room door closed behind them, her entire demeanor changed. Gone was her seeming calm, replaced by concern that prompted her to whisper, "I must speak with you. Did you notice that Mr. Wol—"

"Not here," he said, the abruptness of his order silencing her. "We need privacy. Go fetch your bonnet, then meet me at the rear door. I will have gloves, shears, and a basket waiting."

While the rose fanciers postponed further discussion until they could be alone, no such requirement inhibited the threesome who remained in the red drawing room. The moment the door closed behind the young couple, Mr. Wolcott looked from Lady Baysworth to Mrs. Montford. "Forgive me if I cross the line," he began, his tone a fine blend of reticence and concern, "but after our tea yesterday, when both of you dear ladies treated me quite like an old and valued acquaintance, I feel as though I need not stand upon ceremony with you."

"Certainly you need not," her ladyship replied. "Is that not so, Agatha?"

When their hostess vouchsafed no reply, merely blushed a most becoming shade of pink, her old friend spoke for her. "Agatha feels as I do, sir, that time cannot be allowed to be the only measure of a friendship."

"You are most gracious, ma'am. May I, then, speak freely?"

At her nod of acquiescence, he began. "Actually, ma'am, I wish to ask a rather impertinent question, and it is because of your generosity of spirit that I feel obliged to ask it."

Agatha found her voice. "What is it, Cecil?"

He looked directly at her. "What led you to believe that Miss Townsend might be Lady Baysworth's niece?"

Apparently his hostess did not find the question at all impertinent, for she told him as much of the story as she knew, beginning with Robert's letters to Bow Street and ending with Isobel's agreement to remain with them for a fortnight. She left out only the part involving her son's initial mistrust of Isobel, and the fact that he had felt obliged to kidnap her to bring her to Montford House. "Such a dear, sweet girl," she concluded.

"Yes," Lady Baysworth agreed, "and so like Fiona."

"And yet," the gentleman added, his face schooled to reveal nothing more than disinterested concern, "the young lady maintains that she is not the daughter of the runaway couple. Not the child of your sister and this Byron Smyth."

"Be that as it may," her ladyship said, "she is my niece. A woman knows these things." She placed her hand over her heart. "I can feel it here."

"Forgive me, ma'am, for playing the devil's advocate, but the young lady is a professional actress, and you are a woman in possession of wealth and social position." He refrained from voicing the word "vulnerable," but to himself he admitted the validity of that description.

Lady Baysworth *tsk-tsked* at his obvious innuendo. "I see what you are about, sir. You suspect our Isobel of being a charlatan, but you may believe me when I tell you that she is the soul of honesty. Is she not, Agatha?"

Her friend nodded in agreement. "Isobel does not lie. Not ever. It is a matter of principle with her. Furthermore, far from trying to ingratiate herself with Edith, she has done everything in her power to convince us all that she and Edith are not related. Would a charlatan do that? I think not."

"No," the gentleman agreed quietly, "she would not." To himself he added, "Not unless she was very, very clever."

Isobel made short work of fetching her bonnet, then hurried down the stairs to join Robert. He waited outside for her, near the cucumber vines and the late-blooming rhubarb, a woven basket in his hand. As she drew near he took her arm and led her to the left, doubling back to the side of the house where the formal gardens were laid out.

Actually, the gardens were less formal than they had been in the previous century, when native flowers were deemed of no value and exiled. Gone were the once elaborate configurations that were bordered by uniformly trimmed hedges and rigidly pruned trees—an idealized landscape that acted as a buffer between the house and the wild countryside. Now, the trees had been allowed to grow as nature had intended; a multicolored rock garden circled a lichen-covered fountain; in the sandy, loamy soil the velvet-faced pansies, as well as the lilies, violets, and gladioli, attempted to escape the confines of their beds, as if hoping to mingle with the fragrant thyme that was planted all along the fieldstone walkway.

At the far end of the garden the roses grew. Great mounds of brilliant pink buds covered a six-foot wall, all but obliterating the stacked stone and giving the impression that the wood had been allowed to run wild. In the foreground well-regulated beds of pink and red blooms grew on small trellises. Even at a distance, the fragrance was intoxicating.

"This is the Bouquet d'Or," Robert said, pausing before an exquisite climbing rose. "Can you cut and talk at the same time, or should we repair to that stone bench beside the sundial?"

"I cannot wait a moment longer," Isobel declared, taking the shears and beginning to snip away at the blossoms. "I must tell you what I noticed about Mr. Wolcott."

"Has it to do with his limp?" Robert asked.

She paused in her cutting to stare at him. "You saw?"

"Not at first," he said, "but before you reached the settee it occurred to me that the gentleman looked different, somehow. Only after you said you must speak with me did I realize what had captured my attention. Odd, is it not, that an injury should desert one leg in favor of another?"

"Actually, I believe the supposed accident was said originally to have damaged his right knee. The error was committed yesterday morning when your guest limped to the breakfast table while leaning upon his servant's arm."

"Yes. I recall that at that time it was the left side that seemed to give him pain. Now, of course, we must ask ourselves what prompted him to perpetrate such a fraud. What did he hope to gain?"

"Entrance to Montford House," she said.

"That was, of course, his primary reason, but what does he hope to find here?"

"Or who?" Isobel offered.

"Or who?" Robert concurred.

"Might he be a fortune hunter? You cannot have failed to notice how handsome he is. Perhaps he wishes to ingratiate himself with Mrs. Montford."

The idea caused Robert to stare at her, incredulity writ plainly upon his face. "With Mother!"

"Do not look so surprised. She may be your parent, sir, but she is a very pretty woman. And she is still quite young enough to be swept off her feet by a dashing gentleman."

"Yes, but—"

"I know little of fortune hunters. Is it so unheard of for one of them to pursue a female no longer in her first blush of youth?"

"No," he replied, "but they always pursue females with fortunes. My mother's jointure is no more than adequate for her own needs. I cannot think such a sum would tempt a gentleman of Mr. Wolcott's obviously expensive taste."

That possibility explained away, they remained quiet for some time, each lost in thought, the only sound the metallic *click-click* of the scissors as Isobel absently snipped away at the lovely blossoms of the Bouquet d'Or. Luckily, before she could totally denude the delicate Oriental bush, Robert reached out and caught her hand, removing the scissors from her fingers and taking the overflowing basket from her arm.

"Come," he said, "we can do no more here."

While they retraced their steps past the rock garden that circled the fountain, Robert still held her hand. Then, as they progressed to the beds of native plants and skirted the fragrant thyme that grew all along the stone walkway, he tucked her hand into the crook of his arm. Never having walked thus with a man, Isobel was immediately conscious of the rock-hard forearm beneath her hand, and of the warmth of Robert's body where her arm was pressed against his ribs.

Immediately, the garden with its pleasurable sights and smells all but disappeared, and Isobel was aware of nothing but the man beside her. Even through the thickness of his bottle green coat, she fancied she could feel the slightly rough texture of his taut skin, and the sensation went to her head much as the champagne had done several nights ago. She wanted to look up at him, to see if their proximity were having the same effect upon him, but she dared not, lest she betray her own reactions.

Never having felt even the slightest attraction for any of the men of her acquaintance—most of them actors who held inflated opinions of themselves— Isobel had been quite unprepared for this rather devastating dose of male magnetism. She was even less prepared for her overwhelmingly feminine response to that maleness, and she found herself wondering how it would feel to be swept up into a pair of strong male arms.

No, that was not exactly truthful, for she did not wish to be in just *any* male arms. Isobel wanted to be swept into Robert Montford's arms. She was imagining being crushed to his broad chest when he spoke to her, bringing her thoughts crashing back to earth.

"Well?" he said "What do you think?"

Think? She had lost the power to think. At that moment, with Robert beside her, Isobel could only feel. She was the embodiment of every woman who had ever found herself lost in the wonder of being with a man who made her heart race. A man who made her breath catch in her throat. A man who made her entire body tingle with awareness

"Think?" she finally managed to say. "About what?"

"About our taking a little side trip to the stable."

She must have looked as bemused as she felt, for he said, "I asked if you would care to accompany me to the stable, for I wish to see if Mr. Wolcott's post chaise shows any signs of having hit the rock that supposedly pitched him into the road."

Eight

When Isobel dressed for dinner that evening, she took more time than usual arranging her hair. Giving in to a whim, she pinned her red-gold tresses rather loosely at the back of her head, allowing several wispy tendrils to escape and fall softly at the nape of her neck. Satisfied with the effect, she tied the satin laces of her kidskin slippers, then stepped into her dress. Her wardrobe being limited, she had only the cream-colored sarcenet, but the blond lace that trimmed the small sleeves added a touch of style, and she was honest enough to admit that the simple lines of the dinner dress suited her figure.

She debated the advisability of adding her one piece of jewelry—a clever interlocking of the two dramatic masks of comedy and tragedy—to the square neck of the dress, but at the last minute she decided to forgo the enamel brooch and returned it to its small, satin-lined box. After placing the box in the top drawer of the dressing table, she blew out the candles on the washstand and went belowstairs to join the two ladies and the two gentlemen.

When she entered the music room, where Kendrick had informed her the family would meet for sherry, Isobel found only one of the gentlemen. Unfortunately, it was the one she least wished to encounter.

"Mr. Wolcott," she said, her voice revealing none of the trepidation she felt. "Good evening, sir."

"Miss Townsend," he replied. If this particular gentleman found anything to admire in the arrangement of her hair or the fit of her dress, Isobel saw no indication of it, nor did he show the least pleasure in her company, not even bothering to smile when he greeted her.

Though she requested that he not stand, bidding him spare his injured knee, he paid her no heed but stood and made her an elegant bow.

She would say this for Cecil Wolcott—he might prove to be a rogue of some kind, but he was certainly a fine figure of a man, tall and lean, with the healthy complexion of one who enjoys a bit of exercise and shuns the dual vices of overly-rich food and strong drink. The music room was decorated in shades of maroon and silver, and whether by accident or design Mr. Wolcott complemented the decor, for he wore a burgundy-colored coat with silver knee breeches and a silver-striped waistcoat.

After curtsying to him, Isobel selected a slipper chair on the opposite side of the room from where the gentleman had been sitting.

"Do you play?" he asked.

"What?"

"The pianoforte," he said, indicating the instrument that was mere inches from her chair.

"Oh, yes, I do, though I am far from proficient. My father insisted I be taught, for he thought it necessary to my education."

Mr. Wolcott appeared to find this information

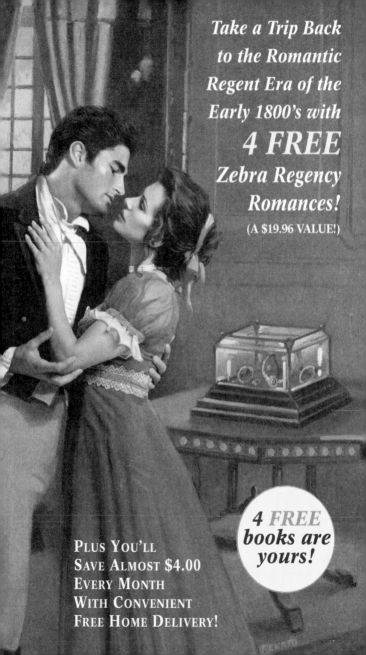

We'd Like to Invite You to Subscribe to Zebra's Regency Romance Book Club and Give You a Gift of 4 Free Books as Your Introduction! (Worth $19.96!)

If you're a Regency lover, imagine the joy of getting 4 FREE Zebra Regency Romances and then the chance to have the lovely stories delivered to your home each month at the lowest prices available! Well, that's our offer to you and here's how you benefit by becoming a Zebra Home Subscription Service subscriber:

- **4 FREE** Introductory Regency Romances are delivered to your doors

- 4 BRAND NEW Regencies are then delivered each month (usually befo they're available in bookstores)

- Subscribers save almost $4.00 every month

- Home delivery is always **FREE**

- You also receive a **FREE** monthly newsletter, *Zebra/ Pinnacle Roman News* which features author profiles, contests, subscriber benefits, bc previews and more

- No risks or obligations...in other words you can cancel whenever yo wish with no questions asked

Join the thousands of readers who enjoy the savings and convenience offered to Regency Romance subscribers. After your initial introductory shipment, you receive 4 brand-new Zebra Regency Romances each month to examine for 10 days. Then, if you decide to keep the books, you'll pay the preferred subscriber's price of just $4.00 per title. That's only $16.00 for all 4 books and there's never an extra charge for shipping and handling.

It's a no-lose proposition, so return the FREE BOOK CERTIFICATE today!

Say Yes to 4 Free Books!
Complete and return the order card to receive this $19.96 value, *ABSOLUTELY FREE!*

(If the certificate is missing below, write to:)
Zebra Home Subscription Service, Inc.,
120 Brighton Road, P.O. Box 5214, Clifton, New Jersey 07015-5214
or call TOLL-FREE 1-888-345-BOOK

FREE BOOK CERTIFICATE

YES! Please rush me 4 Zebra Regency Romances without cost or obligation. I understand that each month thereafter I will be able to preview 4 brand-new Regency Romances FREE for 10 days. Then, if I should decide to keep them, I will pay the money-saving preferred subscriber's price of just $16.00 for all 4...that's a savings of almost $4 off the publisher's price with no additional charge for shipping and handling. I may return any shipment within 10 days and owe nothing, and I may cancel this subscription at any time. My 4 FREE books will be mine to keep in any case.

Name _____

Address _____ Apt. _____

City _____ State _____ Zip _____

Telephone ( ) _____

Signature _____
(If under 18, parent or guardian must sign.)

RG0699

Terms and prices subject to change. Orders subject to acceptance by Zebra Home Subscription Service, Inc.

ZEBRA HOME SUBSCRIPTION SERVICE, INC.

120 BRIGHTON ROAD

P.O. BOX 5214

CLIFTON, NEW JERSEY 07015-5214

AFFIX
STAMP
HERE

quite interesting, and he sat forward in his chair as if not wishing to miss a word. "Your father, you say. He was an actor, was he not?"

Isobel bristled. She did not believe she could endure another scornful remark aimed at those of her profession, especially not from a man who had used questionable methods to gain entrance to the Montfords' home. His post chaise had proved him a liar. As she and Robert had discovered that afternoon in the stables, the wheel of the gentleman's coach showed no sign of ever having encountered a rock.

"To answer your question, sir, my father earned his living on the stage. As to *what* he was, he was above all a gentle and caring man, and the sort of person who never turned from his door anyone who was in need."

If her impassioned speech made any impression upon her listener, he concealed the fact. "He sounds an admirable fellow," Cecil Wolcott said, his voice betraying nothing of what he actually felt. "Mrs. Montford informs me, Miss Townsend, that you have stated unequivocally that your parent was *not* the actor who eloped with Miss Fiona Cochran."

Here was plain speaking, indeed, and Isobel found it difficult to control her temper. "That is true, sir. He was not Byron Smyth, though I fail to see what possible concern that can be of yours."

"Oh, none, I assure you. Still, I could not help wondering if you harbored just the least suspicion that you might be the daughter of Byron Smyth. You are, after all, a beautiful young woman, and from what I have been told by our hostess and dear Lady Baysworth, Byron Smyth was quite handsome."

Isobel could not believe her ears. *How dared he—this, this deceiver—act as if he doubted her word!*

"For all I know of the matter," she said, her voice tight with anger, only just held in check, "Byron Smyth may have been a veritable Adonis, and if so it stands to reason that he and Fiona would have had beautiful children together. Nonetheless, I am not one of them. I cannot say it any plainer than that."

"No," he said, "you cannot. Still—"

Fortunately for Isobel's composure, Robert chose that moment to enter the room. In deference to the occasion, he, too, had donned knee breeches; they were cream satin, as was his waistcoat, and his coat was fashioned of an elegant, dark blue material. Isobel had never seen him look more handsome. Since his arrival was followed only moments later by that of his mother and his godmother, the conversation became much less personal, the topics introduced only those of general interest to a mixed gathering.

After a time, Isobel was able to put aside her annoyance at Mr. Cecil Wolcott and his impertinent questions and allow herself to enjoy the evening. It was just as well that she did not bear him a grudge, for she found herself sitting beside the gentleman at dinner. Robert was at the head of the table, of course, with Isobel seated to his right—a circumstance that lent itself to easy conversation between the two—but the middle-aged gentleman sat to her right, obliging Isobel to speak to him from time to time.

"Isobel, my dear," her hostess said, "what is this I hear about your agreeing to accompany Robert to

Cromer Ridge? Though I trust my son not to allow any accident to befall you, I hope he did explain to you that the ridge requires surefootedness, and a certain amount of nerve."

"She is so like Fiona," Lady Baysworth said, her tone not unlike that of a parent bragging about the feats of her own offspring. "Pluck to the backbone, as my husband was used to say. Afraid of nothing. Let Fiona but hear of some new adventure, and nothing would do her but to give it a try. Always so daring."

The gentleman to Isobel's right made a muffled sound that might have been anything from disagreement with Lady Baysworth's assessment to a simple clearing of his throat. Whatever it was, Isobel chose not to acknowledge that she had heard it. Instead, she addressed her remark to Lady Baysworth, endeavoring to keep her tone light and teasing, as befit the celebration dinner.

"I do not know what you have been told, ma'am, but I am anything but daring. Furthermore, I am persuaded that had you been with us yesterday when we visited The Broads you would not be likening me to your sister, for you would have seen that I am a wretched representative of English womanhood. You may apply to Mr. Montford for a true account of my cowardice when I was all but forced into a leaky old punt."

"Forced?" Agatha Montford said, apparently not as surprised as she might have been to hear the word. "Do you tell me, my dear, that my son is up to his old tricks?"

The gentleman under discussion waved a negligent hand. "Nothing of the kind, Mother. I merely pointed out to Miss Townsend how much she would enjoy the water once she gave over her preconceived notion that there was the least danger involved. And I was correct. Confess it now, Miss Townsend. You were not the least bit afraid."

Isobel assumed the pose of a frightened damsel, her eyes wide and her bottom lip atremble. "I assure you, ma'am, I w-was not the least b-bit afraid. And I cannot w-wait until I am forced—invited, I should say—to c-climb Cromer Ridge."

Though the two ladies laughed aloud at her antics, Robert contented himself with wagging a warning finger at her. He did not laugh, but when he looked at Isobel there was a light of amusement in his eyes that teased while at the same time it invited her to join in the merriment. As she looked into those clear brown orbs Isobel felt a rush of warmth, a sudden, unexpected sense of belonging that left her tingling from head to foot. She allowed herself to enjoy the sensation for several moments before she replied to Mrs. Montford's original remark regarding the need for surefootedness when visiting Cromer Ridge.

"Rest assured, ma'am, that your son has left me in no doubt as to what the future holds in store for me. He has promised me that the climb will require fortitude; he has apprised me of the fact that I will return to Montford House quite shockingly grubby, and shall most likely be denied entrance at the front door; and he has warned me that my reward for these trials will be nothing more than a pocket filled with bugs and other creatures so long dead I will not even know what to call them." After enacting a dramatic shudder, she said, "With such temptations, ma'am, how could I refuse the invitation?"

The ladies laughed again, and the subject was dropped in favor of more general table talk, talk which included Mr. Wolcott. The gentleman proved an informed, and often enthusiastic, conversationalist. After sharing his views upon some of the new farming methods, and expressing his opinions regarding the need for more equitable trade agreements so the poor of the country had access to less expensive food and goods, he surprised Isobel by making a request of her. "I wonder, Miss Townsend, since by your own admission you are not proficient at the pianoforte, if you would give us the pleasure of a recitation this evening?"

"Oh, yes," Lady Baysworth concurred. "Dear Isobel reads beautifully. Only last evening, after bringing me a bowl of quite delicious barley soup, she read to me from Mr. Scott's *Marmion*. I wish you could have heard her, sir, for she put so much feeling into the passages that I felt as though I had been transported to that rugged country. I was quite breathless to see how the adventure would be resolved."

Isobel agreed to do the recitation, but as it turned out she was not the only member of the party to perform. After the gentlemen finished their port and joined the ladies in the music room, with Robert choosing to lean against the mantelpiece and Mr. Wolcott seating himself on the settee next to Agatha Montford, their hostess asked the gentleman if he would favor them with a song or two. "I should be happy to accompany you on the pianoforte."

Encountering the mystified look on her son's face,

she explained her request. "Cecil told Edith and me that he liked nothing better than to join in the singing when among a small party of friends."

As if only just realizing what she had said, the lady blushed and turned to Mr. Wolcott. "That is, sir, if I have not presumed too much, and you do feel as though you are among friends."

"I do indeed," he assured her, flashing her a blinding smile.

If Robert had looked puzzled before, after witnessing the exchange between his mother and their guest, now his face became an unreadable mask, with only his eyes revealing the questions that were going on inside his head. Since he lowered his gaze almost immediately and kept it lowered, Isobel was unable to tell what his thoughts were when his mother sounded a chord then began to play a lively Irish folk tune and the gentleman standing beside the pianoforte lifted his voice, filling the room with a rich, lovely baritone.

The folk tune was followed by a trio of German *lieder* and an Italian art song by Scarlatti, and though Isobel was not as vociferous in her admiration of the soloist as were the other two ladies, honesty compelled her to acknowledge, if only to herself, that his voice was more than pleasing. After an unpretentious rendition of *Weep You No More Sad Fountains* that had Lady Baysworth rummaging in her reticule for a handkerchief to dry her tears, the gentleman closed his performance with *There Is A Lady Sweet And Kind*, a ballad whose familiar, sentimental lyrics prompted her ladyship to sigh romantically and left Agatha Montford gazing at the singer as though he was the sun and the moon all wrapped up in one handsome package.

Only later, after the singer had been congratulated upon his artistry and Isobel had recited two of Shakespeare's sonnets, did she find an opportunity to speak with Robert. "I wonder," she said quietly, "if after this night's work you have reconsidered my theory about Cecil Wolcott being a fortune hunter? Are you still convinced that he is not wishful of fixing his interest with Mrs. Montford?"

Robert looked toward the far end of the music room where his mother stood engaged in animated conversation with her bosom friend and their injured guest, whose limp seemed to have vanished entirely since his musical performance. "I do not know what to think," Robert replied, "but I have this hour and more been composing a letter in my head, a letter to an acquaintance who lives in Sussex. If my friend knows the inhabitants of Wolcott Park, I should like to hear his opinion of Lord Wolcott's younger brother."

"A good idea, sir, but would it not be faster to contact the Bow Street Runners, as you did when seeking information about Fiona's daughter?"

"Perhaps," he replied, a note of reserve in his voice. "Unfortunately, since I first hired the runners I have lost confidence in their loyalty, and for that reason I believe I would be better served to contact my friend."

The next morning, Isobel woke feeling restive and decided that a stroll in the garden might clear the cobwebs from her head. Thinking of nothing more sinister than a look at the roses while the dew still clung to the fragrant petals, she wound her hair into a loose bun at the back of her head, tossed her dark blue cloak around her shoulders, and made her way down the stairs and through the corridor toward the kitchen garden. She had only just opened the rear door and was prepared to step outside into the cool morning air when she heard two voices involved in whispered conversation. One voice was that of Cecil Wolcott; the other was less cultured. Isobel guessed it belonged to the gentleman's valet, the unsociable Mr. Zell.

The men stood on the far side of a thick yew, their figures obscured by the green branches, and one of them held a horse by the reins. Since they had obviously not heard Isobel's approach, she stepped back inside the doorway, where she could listen to their conversation without being observed.

"Here are my letters," Mr. Wolcott said.

"Very well, sir. I'll see the one meant for Lord Wolcott goes with the morning post."

"Good man. And the other letter I shall expect you to deliver personally to Jethro Comstock, who awaits my instructions at The Belled Cat."

"I'll put the missive directly into the Runner's hands, sir. And while I'm in the village, I'll check to see if there's any correspondence waiting for you from Sussex."

"A good idea. My brother said he would write if he had news of any significance. In my letter to him, I related everything I have discovered here. After all, his stake in this affair is every bit as great as my own. Perhaps greater, since he owns Wolcott Park. As his heir, of course, anything that I decide could ultimately affect Wolcott Park."

A sudden rattling of pans in the nearby kitchen made it impossible for Isobel to understand what was said next, and when all was quiet again, the men were discussing someone.

"Considering the hours spent in her company last evening," the servant said, "what think you about the lady?"

"Lady?" The word was filled with contempt.

"The person," his servant corrected.

"I have thought of nothing else but her since we arrived at Montford House, and I tell you truthfully, Zell, the idea of that unworthy female possibly taking my mother's place as mistress of Wolcott Park fairly makes my blood boil."

The horse, apparently sensing anger, whickered and drew his massive head back, obliging the servant to stroke the animal's nose to keep it quiet. "Perhaps it will all come to naught, sir. There may be a letter waiting for you in the village. His lordship may have good news for you, news that'll allow you to leave here and never have to think of her again."

The gentleman sighed. "I pray heaven it is so, and that I may leave this place as I came—alone."

Isobel eased the door shut; she did not wish to hear any more from this would-be deceiver. The situation was worse than she had suspected. From what she had heard, it appeared obvious to her that Cecil Wolcott *was* a fortune hunter determined to win the affections of Robert's mother. His goal, though common enough in society, was despicable, but what bothered Isobel the most was the man's obvious dislike of the lady who was the object of his quest.

"Wicked, wicked man," she said aloud, not the least embarrassed by the fact that she had gained her knowledge by the quite reprehensible act of eavesdropping. "You shall not make a fool of the lady, sir. Not if I can do anything to prevent it."

But what could she do?

Her wisest course of action would probably be to tell Robert what she had overheard and let him handle the situation in whatever way he thought best. Unfortunately, she had firsthand experience of Robert Montford's way of handling things when he thought he was protecting someone he loved—had he not kidnapped Isobel when she would not agree to come to see his godmother, Lady Baysworth? What if she told him everything Wolcott and his servant had said and Robert became so angry he called the man out?

What if he killed Cecil Wolcott?

What if Cecil Wolcott killed Robert!

At that last possibility, Isobel felt a pain that was not unlike having someone put a bullet through her own heart. She had trouble drawing breath into her lungs. How could she bear it if something she said caused Robert to be hurt? How could she bear it if—

Isobel paused, embarrassed at where her thoughts had taken her. Here was foolishness, indeed, for Robert Montford meant nothing to her. Far from it. Her initial reaction to the idea of his being hurt was simply fellow feeling, the kind of sympathy one human would normally feel for another.

If she chose to ignore the fact that her humanitarian instincts had not prompted a similar sympathy for the possible death of Mr. Wolcott, there was nothing marvelous in that. Isobel did not like Cecil Wolcott, while Robert was beginning to figure as one of her friends. She enjoyed his company. They liked one another. It was simple friendship, nothing more complicated than that.

Delighted to have been able to put a name to her fledgling feelings for her host—friendship explained it perfectly!—Isobel eased the door open to see if Wolcott and his servant were still outside. All was quiet. The valet must have mounted his horse and ridden to Gresham to deliver his letter. As for his master, Isobel did not care where he was, just so long as she did not meet him. Assuming that he had walked around to the rose garden, she decided to change her destination to the little brook.

When she had visited the brook four days ago, the tranquility of the rustic bower had brought her a sense of peace. She hoped it would exercise a similar calming effect today, bringing serenity to her agitated thoughts.

After pulling the hood over her head, Isobel closed the door behind her and hurried past the well-tended vegetable garden to the narrow footpath. By the time she had traversed the half mile that ended at the shallow, gently flowing brook, she had decided she would keep to herself what she had overheard. She would watch Wolcott, observing his behavior toward Agatha Montford and the lady's receptivity to his attentions. Then, if it looked as if a serious attachment were forming, she would inform Robert of what had been said.

Praying it would all come to naught, Isobel trod through the carpet of forget-me-nots, this time barely noticing their uncomplicated beauty, and approached the slightly arched bridge. She assumed she was alone, and only after she had stepped upon the moss-covered stones did she notice the stranger who approached from the far bank.

Because of the willow trees that grew down near the water's edge, the man had been hidden from Isobel's view just as she had been hidden from his, but now they stepped upon the bridge at the same time. They both stopped short, each equally startled to see the other.

If the scowl upon the man's unshaven face was anything to go by, he was not pleased to have been discovered. Of course, his displeasure probably had much to do with the slingshot that protruded from his pocket and the brace of wood pigeons that were only partially hidden beneath his dirty smock, pigeons whose once pretty, blue-gray heads now hung limp and lifeless.

Isobel did not doubt for one moment that the fowl rightfully belonged to the owner of the estate, and as she stared at the smallish man with the thin, unsmiling mouth, her heart began to beat painfully against her ribs. He was a poacher, and the penalty for poaching was deportation. With such a threat hanging over his head, a miscreant might not think twice about silencing any witnesses to his crime.

Hard, button-black eyes glowered at Isobel as though she had just been elected the primary cause of all his misfortunes. "What're you doing out here?" he said, his tone both insolent and accusing. "You spying on me?"

She shook her head. "I had no idea anyone was here. I just came to see the brook."

"This here's private property," he said, and the irony of his informing her of that fact very nearly sent Isobel into a fit of nervous laughter. To her relief, she managed somehow to retain her composure.

The belligerent little man took a few steps onto the bridge, then looked her over from the hood that covered her head to the hem of her far-from-new cloak. His stare was unquestionably threatening. "You one of the Montford housemaids?"

Before she could disabuse him of the notion that she was a member of the staff, he waved in the general direction of the house. "You better get on back to work," he said, "and if you know what's good for you you'll forget you ever glimmed eyes on me. You say a word to anyone, and next time you come this way you'll find me waiting here for you, come to show you how I repay them as don't stand my friend."

The man walked toward her, then, his boots sounding loudly on the stone bridge, and though Isobel wanted to back away to give him plenty of room to pass, she dared not let him see that she was frightened. She knew a bully when she saw one, and she knew that to show fear would be to invite further intimidation, so she stood straight and tall, her chin held high.

He made as if to walk on past her, but just as Isobel was breathing a sigh of relief he turned suddenly and caught her by the neck of her cloak, yanking her against him. "Heed my words," he said, his face so close to hers she could smell his rotting teeth. "You better not tell, or you'll pay dear."

Where Isobel had been frightened only moments before, now she was furious—furious that this thief had yanked her around as though she were no more than a sack of rubbish. She was angry that he had threatened her, angry that he was breathing his disgusting breath in her face. "Take your hands off me!"

When he did not obey on the instant, she struck him, dealing him a resounding blow to the side of the head. The slap so surprised the poacher that he let out a yelp and released her.

Not waiting to see what he might do next, Isobel moved out of his reach, stopping only when her backbone came up against the hard stone of the parapet. The bully swore a particularly vile oath, then took a step toward her, his arm drawn across his chest as though he meant to strike her a backhand blow. To ward off the impending retaliation, Isobel blurted out the first thing she could think of that might send him packing. "If you were smart," she said, "you would get away from here as fast as possible, for Mr. Montford stops at the brook every morning to water his horse. If he finds you here bothering me, I believe it will be *you* who pays dearly. The gentleman is larger than you and very strong, and should he choose to do so he could thrash you within an inch of your life."

Her would-be attacker paused, obviously rethinking his plan to strike her. Isobel could see the effect her words had upon him, for the look in his small black eyes was one of impotent fury. Fortunately, at the prospect of dealing with a man—and a large one at that—the poacher's bravery deserted him, and he lowered his arm. He swore again. Then, after slandering Isobel's virtue and her intelligence, he turned and hurried off the bridge, trampling dozens of innocent forget-me-nots in his haste to be gone.

It was a full two minutes before Isobel's heart quit

hammering against her ribs and her breath slowed down to something resembling its normal pace. Even so, she shook all over like a *blanc mange*, and she was obliged to lean against the parapet to keep her knees from buckling beneath her. She had never been so frightened in her life, and she thanked heaven that she had survived the encounter with the poacher. He had threatened her and manhandled her, but she might have fared much worse, and she knew it.

Still trembling, but longing for the security of the house, Isobel decided her legs were strong enough to support her for the half mile walk back up to the path.

She had only just let go her hold on the parapet when she heard a *whirring* noise, and a missile of some sort hit her on the back of the head. The object had traveled at great speed, and the pain of the blow was excruciating, making her feel as if her brain had splintered into a million pieces.

For a moment Isobel thought she might have been shot. That assumption proved false, however, for while she held her hand to her aching head, dazed yet sensible enough to thank heaven that her hood had softened the blow somewhat, the toe of her boot struck a large, smooth pebble that had not been on the bridge earlier.

Isobel stared at the pebble, which lay there looking quite innocent. Looks could be deceiving, of course, and though the weapon was not a bullet it had been most effective. To add to her distress, logic told her that this was no accident.

Someone had meant to hit her. But who? And where was that person now?

Certain of only one thing—that she wanted to leave the bridge where she was in full view—Isobel turned to flee. Unfortunately, before she took even one step, she heard another *whir*, and a second rock struck her on the forehead, just above her right eye.

This time, her brain did more than splinter—it very nearly exploded.

Isobel moaned, but the sound seemed to come from a long way off, almost as if it had little to do with her. A most unnerving array of colored spots blurred her vision, and while she fought to contain her rising panic, the bridge seemed to sway beneath her feet. She reached out, trying to find the parapet, something to hold on to until she could regain her equilibrium. All was in vain, for within moments she was swallowed up in unrelieved darkness.

Without uttering another sound, Isobel fell unconscious to the hard stone floor of the bridge.

Nine

Robert pulled Ajax to a stop, surprised to discover his houseguest on the footpath that led to the stone bridge. Whether the early bird was going to or coming from that spot was not immediately apparent. Only one thing was clear—from the look of annoyance on the man's face, he was not pleased to have been observed.

Curious to know why the gentleman was abroad so early and why he did not wish to be seen, Robert dismounted and dropped the reins, allowing the horse to find his own way to the brook for his morning drink. "Good morning, sir," he called.

Cecil Wolcott schooled his features into a smile of welcome and touched the tip of his forefinger to the brim of his stylish gray beaver. "Good day to you," he replied. "I had not thought to see anyone else out so early."

That much, Robert decided, was obvious! "I ride most mornings," he said, then offered no further comment. He merely looked expectantly toward the other man, whose smile had slipped just a bit, betraying his continued vexation. It was not like a gentleman of Mr. Wolcott's social aplomb to fidget with his cravat, and since he was doing so at the moment, running his finger beneath the knot and then straightening the ends of the linen, Robert was interested to see if he could discover just what had disturbed the man's usual calm.

Unconcerned that his behavior was rude in the extreme, Robert remained silent, allowing the awkward moment to stretch between them. It was his guest who finally broke the silence.

"I felt in need of a breath of air," he said, "and a bit of mild exercise."

"Ah, yes. Air and exercise. The universal panaceas. You found them beneficial to an injured knee, did you?"

Cecil Wolcott's mouth narrowed as if in anger, but when he replied his tone remained convivial. "I hope they may prove to be so, though as with most remedies, only time will prove their efficacy."

Not willing to let the man relax just yet, Robert said, "I really must congratulate you."

"Oh? How is that, Mr. Montford? I vow I cannot call to mind anything I have done that merits recognition."

"You are too modest, sir, for your recovery from the injury caused by the carriage accident has been nothing short of miraculous. Why, looking at you just then, traversing the footpath that leads to the brook, I found it difficult to discern which of your knees had been hurt. The limp is all but gone."

The man's eyes darkened, and Robert wondered at his guest's continued control in view of such obvious provocation.

"I had no idea there was a brook," Cecil Wolcott said, apparently having decided to end their little verbal contest. "If it is not too great a distance, I should like to see it." He stared pointedly at Robert, all but daring him to resume his poorly veiled innuendos. "Are you bound there yourself? If so, may I join you? That is, if I do not intrude."

Robert would have liked to inform the gentleman that his very presence at Montford House was an intrusion upon the family, but he kept such thoughts to himself. It behooved him to find out as much as possible about this stranger who was their guest, and it could be that a quiet morning stroll would be just the thing for discovering a few facts.

"I understand," he said once they had fallen into step together, "that you are from Sussex."

"That is where I was born, and where I make my home. Wolcott Park belongs to my brother, but I do what I can to assist him in managing the estate."

"And is the management of someone else's estate an occupation you enjoy? Or have you aspirations for a place of your own?"

It was an impertinent question, but Robert wanted to know the answer, for his mother's sake. If this man were, indeed trying to gain his mother's good opinion—along with her widow's portion—Robert needed to be on the alert. To his surprise, the gentleman did not take offense—either that, or he was as good an actor as their other guest, Miss Isobel Townsend.

"Actually," Cecil Wolcott said, "in my youth, I had aspirations of an entirely different sort. I considered estate management and everything about country life a dead bore. At that time I longed for adventure, travel, gaiety."

"And now?"

"Now," he said, "I find the quiet life perfectly

suits my taste. My brother and I rub along reasonably well together, and though I should like to have a place I might manage exactly as I like, trying my hand at a few of the more modern techniques of farming, I have no complaints."

"None?" Robert said.

"None save those I share with other men who, like me, have reached their middle years and have neither wife nor child to add happiness and promise to their future years."

Robert found his answer irritating in the extreme. "And is that what you wish, sir? A wife to brighten your future years? Preferably one in possession of an estate that would become yours once the marriage vows were exchanged?"

What his guest would have answered to that insulting question, Robert never discovered, for while he spoke they had drawn close to the brook, where the horse stood at the water's edge, sipping from the gently moving water. As it turned out, Robert paid no more attention to the horse than he did to the man beside him, for his interest was fairly caught by something he spied midway on the stone bridge. It was a bundle of some sort, a bundle covered over by a dark blue wrap. As Robert stared, it occurred to him that the blue material was vaguely familiar.

"What is it?" Mr. Wolcott asked, looking toward the bridge as well. "What do you see?"

"I am not certain, but I—" The words had no sooner left his mouth than Robert recognized the blue wrap. It belonged to Isobel; it was the cloak she had worn the night he brought her to Montford House. Seized by a sudden premonition, Robert hurried toward the bridge, his long strides taking him there in a matter of seconds. As he drew closer, the bundle became what it was—a cloak with someone lying frighteningly still beneath it.

He knew, though he tried to deny his knowledge, that the someone was Isobel Townsend.

Something hard and painful seemed to stick in Robert's throat, and when he bent to remove the cloak and saw the young woman—her face deathly pale, with a trickle of blood that began at her forehead and ran down her cheek—the pain in his throat relocated to his chest. "Isobel," he whispered. "Isobel, can you hear me?"

She did not answer, nor did she move, and though Robert bid her open her eyes she did not obey.

"Wolcott," he yelled, "catch my horse and bring him here."

"What is it? What have you discovered?"

"Damnation, man! This is no time for questions. Do as I say."

While Cecil Wolcott walked down to the water's edge and caught Ajax's reins, Robert put his arms beneath Isobel and lifted her ever so carefully, gently holding her against his chest so that her head might rest in the hollow of his shoulder. She moaned, but that was the only sound she made. Still, Robert offered a word of gratitude that she gave any response at all. Whatever had happened to her, she was still alive.

In order to mount the horse Robert was obliged to give Isobel into Wolcott's keeping, but once he was in the saddle he reached down and reclaimed her. He settled her safely in front of him, his left arm around her waist to hold her fast. Then, with the reins in his right hand, he urged the horse forward, keeping him at a trot for the few minutes needed to reach the kitchen garden.

Fortunately, just as horse, rider, and the unconscious Isobel arrived one of the kitchen maids came out to pick some vegetables. Though the servant screamed when she saw the blood that stained the front of Robert's shirt and waistcoat, she retained enough sense to go to the horse's head while her master dismounted and then lifted the injured lady down. With Isobel in his arms once more, her forehead resting against his neck, Robert felt the warm moisture of her blood upon his skin. The jostling of the horseback ride must have opened her wound, for now it bled profusely.

Robert had thought he was frightened earlier, but now, with Isobel's blood virtually pouring from her body, he felt as if some unknown force had reached inside him and was squeezing the very air from his lungs.

"Go to stables," he told the maid, "and send someone to the village for the apothecary."

The maid bobbed a curtsy. "Y-yes, sir. Right away, sir."

"And tell them to hurry!"

Knowing the maid would do as she was bid, Robert lost no time in entering the kitchen. He ignored both the scullery maid's gasp of surprise and Cook's hysterical petition to the saints to bless them all in their hour of need, choosing to hurry along the corridor and up the stairs. He did not stop until he had kicked open the door to Isobel's bedchamber, crossed the room in three long strides, and laid her down on the pale pink counterpane, employing infinite care as he slipped his arms from beneath her.

"Isobel," he said, "can you hear me?"

When she did not respond Robert brushed aside a lock of reddish-blond hair that had stuck to her blood-soaked forehead. Then he reached inside his waistcoat, found his handkerchief, and placed the folded linen on the wound, applying pressure to stanch the flow.

It was not to be marveled at that the commotion of his unorthodox arrival had alerted the entire household to the fact that something serious had happened. Within less than a minute Lady Baysworth appeared at the bedchamber door, her breathing labored, as though she had come at a run.

"Robert," she demanded, "what can you mean by coming into Isobel's room this way? I heard you kick the door open, and I—Oh, dear heaven," she said, spying Isobel at last and rushing to her bedside. "Oh, my poor girl. Is she . . . ?" The question seemed to stick in her throat, and as tears pooled in her eyes Robert reached out with his free hand and squeezed her arm.

"Isobel is alive," he said, "but she has lost a lot of blood. I can tell you no more than that."

"But what mishap befell her? How came she to be so grievously injured?"

"I cannot tell you that, either."

"You were not with her when this occurred?"

Robert shook his head. "It was by chance that I found her. I stopped to give Ajax his morning drink at the brook, and when I approached the stone footbridge I saw Isobel lying there. She was unconscious when I reached her."

He lifted the folded handkerchief and, seeing that the flow of blood had lessened, he went to the washstand, where a fresh towel hung above the basin. Snatching up the cloth, he brought it back to replace the blood-soaked handkerchief.

"What can I do?" Lady Baysworth asked.

"Fetch your woman," he said, "for she has skill in the sickroom. Tell her to bring bandages and anything else she may deem appropriate."

"I have brought Zell," Cecil Wolcott said from the doorway.

Robert gave scant attention to the valet who stood beside his master, but his gaze did linger for a moment on Wolcott. To have gained the house in such record time, the man must have run the entire half mile. It was an impressive feat for a person with a supposedly injured knee. Robert put that from his mind for the moment. For now, Isobel's health was all that mattered.

"Zell was for many years in the army," Wolcott said when Robert did not accept his offer of help. "You may take my word that he is adept at tending wounds."

Unable to think of any better plan, Robert stepped away from the bed, though he made it perfectly clear that he had no intention of leaving the room while the man administered to Isobel. "Until the apothecary arrives," he said, "I will accept assistance from anyone who can help Miss Townsend."

Approval given, the valet went to the washstand and poured a basin of water. After bringing it and a washcloth to the bed table, he unfastened Isobel's cloak, pushed the hood out of the way, and began bathing her forehead.

Lady Baysworth was the first to notice the blood at the back of Isobel's head. "Robert! Look," she said, her voice none too steady. "There is a second injury. My poor dear Isobel."

Robert hurried to the far side of the bed. There was a mere trace of blood, but he examined the area carefully. A large bump was growing beneath Isobel's hair, but otherwise the wound did not appear serious. Whatever—or whoever—had done this to her, she could thank the combined padding of the hood of the cloak and the thick knot of hair, which was fashioned rather low on her head, for they had softened the blow.

"How can this have happened?" her ladyship asked. "Did she fall, do you suppose?"

Robert was obliged to bite back the angry words that came to mind. This was no fall—he was certain of that—but it would serve no purpose to upset his godmother even more than she was at the moment. Forcing his voice to a calmness that was the antithesis of his true feelings, he said, "Whatever occurred, ma'am, I will get to the bottom of it. I promise you that."

The valet's sponging of Isobel's face was having a salubrious effect upon her, and she began to moan. As well, her eyelids fluttered several times, then opened. At first she seemed unable to focus those blue eyes, and she stared in a somewhat dazed fashion at the crowd surrounding her bed. When she lifted her hand to her head, as if to discover for herself why the valet was bathing her face with such care, Robert caught her fingers just in time and held them instead.

"Be still," he said, his voice firm yet gentle. "Believe me, it is for the best."

She looked at him, then at one expectant face

after another, finally returning her gaze to Robert. "Why are you all staring at me?" she asked. "Please, tell me what has happened."

Robert spoke softly. "We had hoped you might tell us. Do you remember anything about how you received your injuries?"

"I am injured? Is that why my head aches so dreadfully?"

"I should think it is," he replied. He spoke in what he hoped was a reassuring manner, while at the same time he held her hand between both of his, willing some of his strength into her. "I have sent for Mr. James, the apothecary, who should arrive soon. After the fellow tends your wounds, he can give you a draught to ease your present discomfort. In the meantime, if you can, tell me anything you remember about being on the bridge."

Confusion clouded her lovely eyes. "I remember getting dressed this morning," she said, "and coming down the stairs. But I can recall nothing else. Did I walk to the brook? I have no recollection of it."

When the effort to remember made her crease her forehead, causing her to cry out at the pain, Robert bid her put all else from her thoughts. "Never mind," he said. "There will be time enough for questions after you have been seen to properly. Once you have had a chance to rest, I am confident your memory will return."

As it transpired, the details of her sojourn to the brook and the subsequent mishap remained a mystery for the rest of the day, with only bits and pieces of the puzzle coming back to Isobel. Not that she had a moment's peace in which to fit those pieces together, for the apothecary gave explicit instructions that under no circumstances was she to be allowed to sleep for the next two hours, and after he left her she received a steady stream of visitors, all of them intent upon keeping her awake.

Once the requisite two hours were accomplished, Lady Baysworth shooed everyone from the bedchamber, and though she seated herself in the small pink slipper chair, refusing to budge from the room, she sat quietly, allowing Isobel to snuggle beneath her covers and close her eyes. Within moments, Isobel had surrendered to blessed sleep.

She woke several times during the next hours, each time feeling groggy and disoriented. Each time she discovered a different person sitting in the slipper chair, ready to offer her a drink and assure her that all was well. Lady Baysworth was replaced by Agatha Montford, who must have given over to Meg. Isobel did not question their being there, keeping watch over her, for it was comforting to know that someone cared, comforting not to be alone.

At one time, she awoke to find the room in semidarkness. Only one small candle was lit, and it reposed on the mantel across the room. Though she tried to focus her eyes, Isobel could not determine who occupied the chair. She soon gave up the effort, for her head ached excruciatingly, and when she turned it, seeking a cool spot on the pillow, a shaft of pain shot through her and she cried out.

Immediately, someone was at her side. Large, firm hands checked the bandage around her head, and as he leaned close Isobel recognized the clean, spicy aroma of Robert's shaving soap.

"Are you in pain?" he asked, his voice husky with

sleep. It was a comforting sound—comforting and pleasantly intimate.

"Just a little," she replied.

"The apothecary left some drops in case you needed something for the pain. I can give them to you, if you like."

"Yes, please."

He turned to the bed table and picked up a small green vial, unscrewing the top as he spoke. "Would you prefer the drops in water, or stirred into some of the lemonade Cook sent up?"

"Water," she replied, her voice sounding feeble in her own ears, "but do not tell Mrs. Nidby I refused her lemonade."

"I promise," he said. A smile pulled at the corners of his mouth, and Isobel smiled in return. At least she *thought* she smiled—her body seemed to be composed of parts that did not necessarily respond to the commands of her brain.

"Here," Robert said, slipping his arm beneath her shoulders, "let me help you to sit up so you can drink without mishap. I am not very good at this nursemaid business, so it will require the efforts of us both if you are to drink the concoction without spilling half the contents of the glass on your person."

"I will do my best," she said."

"Good girl. Here we go."

He lifted her into a sitting position, then sat beside her so that her head rested on his shoulder. When he raised the glass to her lips, she drank thirstily. The liquid felt good going down her gullet, and once she had drunk at least half the contents of the glass, she found she felt much better. It crossed Isobel's mind that her improved health might be a result of leaning against Robert's reassuring chest. She would have liked to remain as she was, nestled against him, with his strong arm around her, but as soon as he returned the glass to the bed table he eased her back onto the pillows.

The drops began to take effect immediately, and Isobel felt herself slipping into oblivion. Before she floated away entirely, however, she wanted to thank Robert for being there. "You do quite well as a nursemaid, sir."

"Thank you," he said, tucking the cover back around her shoulders. "Now you be a good patient and go back to sleep."

"Yes. I will."

There was something more she wanted to tell him, something important, something about a duel between him and Cecil Wolcott, but her brain was going all fuzzy and she could not remember clearly. "Robert," she said, her voice edged with panic, "do not fight the duel. Please. I am afraid for you. I do not want you to be shot."

He stared at her for a moment as though surprised at her words, then reached down and placed his hand against her face. "Shh. Rest now."

Robert's broad palm cupped her cheek, and while his fingertips moved slowly back and forth at her temple, fairly mesmerizing her with their gentle touch, a fire of some sort darkened his eyes. Unfortunately, Isobel was too sleepy to identify the cause of that fire.

"Do not worry," he said, the words almost inaudible. "If it will make you rest easier, I will promise to avoid duels altogether."

"Thank you." Reassured, she snuggled her face

into his palm. "Umm. You have wonderful hands. So warm. So strong. I like the way they feel against . . ."

There was so much more she wanted to say, but her tongue refused to cooperate, and within a matter of moments she drifted away completely.

Isobel slept until early afternoon of the next day, at which time she awoke feeling decidedly better. The pain in her forehead was now little more than a dull throb, and when the apothecary removed the bandage he declared her wound to be healing nicely and covered it with a simple sticking plaster.

After Mr. James left, Meg came to help Isobel wash up a bit and change into a pretty, lace-trimmed nightrail and wrapper Agatha Montford had sent up as a get well gift. Once the maid had laid a handsome red and blue India shawl across Isobel's lap, she began to brush out the long, reddish-blond tresses, being careful not to cause the patient any added distress. She had only just finished braiding the thick hair into a loose plait when there was a knock at the door.

The visitor was Lady Baysworth, who held a letter crushed to her breast. From the tearstains on the lady's cheeks, it was obvious the missive contained momentous news.

"Ma'am," Isobel said, "what is amiss?"

Her ladyship smiled and resorted to the handkerchief in her hand, swiping at newly fallen tears. "Amiss? My dear child, nothing is amiss. In fact, everything is perfect, for I have had the most wonderful news." She held the letter out for a moment, sighed, kissed the paper, then pressed it to her bosom once again. "I have had a letter from Gordon."

Isobel proceeded carefully, afraid her brain might be playing her false. The only Gordon she knew anything of was Lady Baysworth's son, and he was dead, killed six months ago in the Peninsula. "Your pardon, ma'am, but did you say your letter was from—"

"Gordon," the lady said, unable to contain her joy. "It is from my son! He is alive!"

Ten

"My son was, indeed, shot," Lady Baysworth related once she had regained her composure, "but he was not killed. Here," she said, "allow me to read to you from Gordon's own words."

My Dear Mother,
 I know you must be beside yourself wondering why I have not written. I took a bullet in the shoulder, but I wish you will not worry, for I have received excellent care and am well on my way to a complete recovery. After our defeat at the battle of Corunna, I was taken aboard ship to a field hospital in the south of Portugal. That was in late January, and for some time things there were in such chaos that letter writing was not given a high priority.
 Now, here it is Easter, and we have been informed that mail will be collected tomorrow. I hope you receive this letter before many weeks pass, and that I will not be late in wishing you a happy birthday.

Lady Baysworth paused, her voice now heavy with emotion. "My birthday was the middle of June, and it is now almost the end of July. Only think how long this letter has taken to reach me. What agonies I suffered, believing my child killed. Believing that I would never see him again. Never hold him in . . . in my arms. Never—"

"But how wonderful, ma'am, that word has come at last. I cannot tell you how happy I am for you. And for Lieutenant Baysworth, as well. Does he say if he will be coming home?"

The question successfully stopped the tears that had welled up once more in the lady's eyes. "He informs me that the army will begin sending the wounded back to England as soon as adequate ships become available." She sighed. "Only think of it, my dear. My Gordon is alive, and he may well be on his way home to me even as we speak."

"I pray his return is swift, ma'am."

They spoke for some little time, with the ecstatic mother regaling Isobel with stories of Gordon Baysworth's baby years, his infancy, and his growth to manhood. The lady's joy and thanksgiving kept the stories from becoming a bore, but Isobel was not sorry when her ladyship recalled the need to send word to her own household, informing the staff that Lieutenant Baysworth might be arriving home at any time.

After her visitor left, Isobel napped for a time, but she was roused from that gentle sleep by a knock at her bedchamber door. "Come in," she called. The visitor was Meg, and to Isobel's delight the maid carried a tea tray laden with a steaming pot, cups, a dinner plate filled with tiny sandwiches, and a smaller plate piled high with freshly-baked seed cakes. The warm, spicy aroma of the cakes drifted to Isobel's nose, inspiring her to breathe deeply. "Yum. That smells delicious."

"It does, indeed," a deep, masculine voice said. "May I join you for tea?"

The food was forgotten as Isobel looked toward the door, her heart racing at the sound of Robert Montford's voice. She had not seen him since the night before, when he had held her close so she might drink her medicine. Later he had touched her face, and the memory of his fingertips caressing her temple sent a shiver of delight up her spine.

"Well?" he asked when she did not answer. "Shall I stay or go?"

Telling herself not to act like a fool, Isobel bid him come in. "I should enjoy sharing my tea with you."

"Actually," he said, "the boot is on the other foot, for it is I who am sharing my tea with you. If Mrs. Nidby had her way, you would be partaking of a bowl of thin gruel and a cup of warm barley water."

Isobel pretended a shudder. "In light of your generosity of spirit, sir, what can I say?"

"A simple, 'Thank you' will do for a start."

"Thank you," she said, "for saving me."

"From what?" he asked, a smile lighting his eyes. "Gastronomical boredom?"

"That, and from whoever attacked me on the footbridge."

All amusement gone from his visage, Robert motioned her to silence. Turning toward the maid, who was busy arranging their meal on the small table by the window, he said, "That will be all, Meg. You may return to the kitchen."

The gossip-loving servant's disappointment was obvious from the crestfallen look on her face, but she obeyed quickly enough, curtsying and leaving the room. Since the door had been left open for propriety's sake, Robert waited until Meg was out of hearing before he returned his attention to Isobel. "You have remembered something."

"Everything," she replied, "except the identity of the person who wished me harm. Regrettably, that piece of information remains a mystery."

Their tea forgotten, Robert pulled up a chair beside the bed and bid her tell him what she could of yesterday's events. Happy to unburden herself, Isobel told him the entire story, beginning with her eavesdropping on the conversation between Cecil Wolcott and his valet and ending with her encounter with the poacher.

Ignoring Robert's muttered oath, Isobel did her best to describe the man on the bridge. "He was a small, petulant-looking fellow, unshaven, with a thin, unsmiling mouth."

"Willem Potter," Robert said, his own mouth set in angry lines."

"You know him?"

"Potter is one of my tenants. At least, he is for the moment. It needed only this for me to rid myself of the troublesome creature."

"Whoever he might be," Isobel continued, "the man threatened me with unnamed violence should I tell anyone about seeing him. I cannot say for certain, though, that it was he who hurled the stone at me. It was a stone, was it not?"

"Yes. I found a rather large pebble on the bridge. It was red with your blood."

The word made Isobel shiver.

"Unfortunately, the stone was not the only thing I found on or near the bridge."

When she asked him to explain his words, Robert told her about meeting their supposedly injured guest on the footpath halfway between the brook and the house. "As luck would have it, it was impossible to tell which was his destination. At that time, Wolcott claimed to be unaware of the existence of the brook, and I have no proof that he spoke anything but the truth.

"Still, he might have discovered that you overheard him talking to the valet. In all honesty, however, though you and I might find his conversation insulting, the content was hardly damaging enough to make him wish to prevent you from telling anyone what you had learned."

"Of course," Isobel added almost as an afterthought, "the gentleman does not like me, not one bit."

Robert's only response was an eyebrow raised in question.

"I have no idea why he does not like me, but it is true nonetheless. And though I have searched my brain for something I have done—some careless word or slight I might be guilty of—I can think of nothing." She paused for a moment, as if embarrassed to continue. "This will sound strange, Robert, but—"

"Never mind how it sounds. Out with it. This is no time for restraint."

"Very well," she said. "I believe that Cecil Wolcott arrived at Montford House with his mind already made up about me, though I swear he and I have never met, and I never even heard his name until the evening he arrived."

Isobel looked to see Robert's reaction to her statement, and to her relief he appeared to consider it significant. "The man is an enigma," he said. "Of course, we have known that about him from the onset. You say he does not like you, and I trust your instincts in the matter. The riddle we must solve now is, does he dislike you enough to do you bodily injury? And while we ponder that, we must not forget Willem Potter, who dislikes everyone."

To hide the dismay she felt at the knowledge that either of two men might have wished her harm, Isobel tried to make light of the situation. "It appears that I possess a rather unenviable talent."

"And what, pray, might that be?"

"Why, only that I have but to come into a neighborhood and all the men turn violent. First there was you, kidnapping me off the streets. Now this, an attack by person or persons unknown. Where, I wonder, will it end?"

Robert understood what she was trying to do, and he allowed her to lighten the tone of the conversation. Pretending to be offended, he said, "There you go, madam, using that word again. Kidnapped, indeed. I have explained that little *contretemps* to you until I am quite blue in the face with the effort. I was merely assisting you into my carriage, as any gentleman would do."

"Ha! The word *gentleman* sits ill upon your tongue, sir. Would a gentleman have so tossed me into his carriage? I think not. 'Tis the action of some loutish farmer who wishes to load an obstinate pig into a wagon."

Robert's lips twitched. "Interesting, madam, that you should mention obstinate pigs. Not that I make any comparisons, of course."

"Naturally not," she said, a smile not far from her own lips. "Everyone who knows me must agree that I am the soul of agreeableness. Why, when I was but a girl, my father was often heard to say that I was the most amiable person of his acquaintance. Never arguing. Always agreeable."

"Yes, yes. Sugar and spice. I did not believe it the first time you said it, and I do not believe it now." When she would have protested, he held up his hand to silence her. "What say you, ma'am, that we abandon this topic and set ourselves to making a few of those sandwiches disappear? I am famished. What of you?"

"Starved," she said. Then, with a giggle, "See how *agreeable* I am?"

Robert pretended not to hear that last. Instead, he crossed to the small table and lifted it, prepared to bring it over to the bed.

"Please," Isobel said, "I should like to sit by the window. I feel as if I have been in bed a month, and I have lost all sense of time. I am not altogether certain what day it is."

"It is Friday, the twenty-first day of July. Though I fail to see what difference the date makes."

"It makes a great deal of difference to me, for I shall be gone in four days' time."

Robert looked at her as though she had spoken in some obscure dialect of Chinese. "What do you mean, gone?"

Isobel did not really want to answer, for merely broaching the subject of her departure had brought a lump to her throat that seemed likely to choke her. "When Monday comes," she replied, "I must leave for Town." When he said nothing, she added,

"You did promise to put me on the stage to London once my two-week visit came to an end. I have a contract at The Haymarket Theater beginning the first week in August. Had you forgotten?"

After a rather protracted silence, he replied, "Yes, as a matter of fact, I had. Foolish of me, I suppose."

He gazed out the bedchamber window for a full two minutes. Then he turned rather abruptly and approached the bed. "The view out that window is of the stone bridge, and I should think you have had quite enough of that scenery for a while. Therefore, if you wish to eat beside a window, perhaps another aspect would be more to your liking."

Before she knew what he meant to do he had scooped her up into his arms, India shawl and all, and was headed out the bedchamber door. To her surprise, he strode to the rear of the corridor and climbed the service stairs to the next floor, all the while carrying her as though her weight was insignificant.

After climbing the stairs two at a time, Robert was not even breathing hard. The same could not be said for Isobel, however, for her breath seemed to be coming in short, erratic puffs, as though she had run a mile. As well, her heart thumped against her chest, and her entire body tingled with awareness of the masculinity of the man who held her in his arms. Obeying an impulse she dared not question, she wrapped her arms around his broad shoulders and laid her head against his neck.

Robert stopped at the rear of the landing, where a pair of rosewood corner chairs that must have gone out of fashion a good fifty years earlier flanked a similarly dated mahogany library table with a green, tooled leather writing pad. Since the furniture was no longer stylish enough for the rooms belowstairs, Isobel surmised that the attraction was the view from the window, and in this she was correct.

Beyond the leaded panes stretched a parkland that had been allowed to go rustic, and in the distance a dozen or so shire horses grazed the green lawns. Not that Isobel cared a fig about the lawns, the shire horses, or the magnificent view; all she could think of was the thrill of being in Robert's arms.

If he had seemed angry before, once they reached the upper-landing window, his temper grew more tranquil. Furthermore, he did not set her in one of the corner chairs, as she had expected, but continued to hold her in his arms. "I like this view," he said.

"Yes," she agreed, "it is beautiful."

While they enjoyed the bucolic scene in companionable silence, Robert rested his chin against the top of her head. Isobel was certain he must be lost in thought and unaware of what he did, for moments later she felt his lips brush her temple. "The nursery is on this floor," he said, "and when I was a lad, I spent many a rainy day gazing out this window."

In need of something that would distract her from imagining those firm lips finding their way down to hers, Isobel said, "Did you chant, 'Rain, rain, go away?' "

Her question made him chuckle. "Naturally, for what boy would choose to be indoors when he might be outside discovering the world?"

"None, I should imagine." As if unable to stop herself, Isobel looked up at him, fully aware that her expression might be thought provocative. "And what of now?" she asked. "Would you rather be outside at this moment?"

Robert's answer was to lower his head, allowing his lips to brush ever so lightly against hers. "At this moment," he said softly, "I am exactly where I wish to be."

"As am I," she replied, tightening her hold around his neck and offering him her mouth once again.

The blood began to pound in Robert's veins, and as he gazed into that lovely face, the lips so full, so soft, so kissable, the blue eyes darkened by innocent passion, newly awakened, all rational thought left his brain. He could think of nothing but his need to cover her mouth with his own. Unfortunately, before he was able to claim those willing lips, he heard someone climbing the service stairs.

"Damnation," he said, not able to stop the oath.

A hint of rose stained Isobel's cheeks, but Robert was unsure whether the color resulted from her being caught in an embarrassing situation or from disappointment at having been denied their kiss. He wanted to think it was the latter. For his own part, had his hands been free, Robert would have gladly tossed the intruder through the window.

"Begging your pardon, sir," one of the footmen said, pausing on the top step.

Robert kept his back to the servant to shield Isobel from the man's sight. "What is it, Benjamin?"

"Mrs. Montford sent me in search of you and Miss Townsend, sir. She wanted you to know that she is sending out cards for a party this evening, inviting a few of the neighbors to come celebrate the happy news of Lieutenant Baysworth's imminent return to his family and friends."

Eleven

Isobel received a visitor scarce half an hour before time for the dinner guests to arrive, and to her relief the visitor was not Robert. For the past two hours, since that peace-disturbing creature had carried her back to her bedchamber, she had been vacillating between hoping he would return to speak with her and praying he would not. Not that she knew what she would say if he did return, for since that brief kiss her senses had been in total upheaval, and any similarity between herself and a rational woman was purely coincidental.

All she could think of was Robert, and the way his lips had felt when they brushed against hers—so soft and gentle—and the way *she* had felt in his arms—as if she had finally found her home. Never had she experienced such warmth, or such excitement. Being there with Robert, being held close against him, having him kiss her, and knowing he wanted to kiss her again, had been heaven. Unfortunately, the arrival of the footman who had been sent to find them had brought them too abruptly to earth.

The presence of the servant had prevented the kiss that had promised to be the most wonderful experience of Isobel's life. How she had wanted that kiss! Had it not been denied her, she would have had two soul-stirring memories, and in the years that lay ahead she might have drawn upon those memories, recalling their sweetness from time to time and reliving the moments, savoring them, letting them warm her heart. However, the opportunity had been missed.

Because she had been deprived of that second kiss, the first one became all the more meaningful, especially when she knew that she and Robert would never—must never—be in one another's arms again. She must not allow it to happen, and not just because she would be leaving in a matter of days.

Isobel Townsend was an actress, a young woman obliged to make her own way in the world, and for an actress and a wealthy gentlemen like Robert Montford only one sort of relationship was possible, a clandestine liaison. Though such an arrangement promised ecstasy for a time, it was a limited time, and it was not for Isobel. Eventually, a temporary liaison would rob her of her very soul. She could not, would not, live a lie.

She loved Robert. She had realized that the evening before when she awoke and found him sitting in the slipper chair, watching over her while she slept. She loved him with all her heart and all her mind, and she would not cheapen that love by settling for some tawdry affair. Once she left Montford House, she was resolved never to see Robert again.

For now, however, her departure was three days hence, and until that day arrived Isobel would allow herself the joy of spending every available minute with the man she loved. That resolution made, she smiled a welcome to her visitor.

"May I come in?" Agatha Montford asked.

"Please do."

Isobel could not help admiring her hostess as she crossed the room toward the slipper chair. The lady looked lovely this evening, dressed in a dinner gown of a coppery georgette that warmed her fair complexion while it flattered her slender figure. A pretty woman, Agatha Montford was always in good looks, but tonight there was an added quality to her beauty—some elusive something that added a sparkle to her hazel eyes.

"How are you, my dear?"

"Physically, ma'am, I am recovered. As to my mental state, I am bored with this forced inactivity, and until you arrived I was bemoaning my fate. In fact, I had been recalling the trip to Cromer Ridge your son and I had discussed several days ago, and I wondered if tomorrow would suit his schedule."

"Tomorrow! But, my dear, the apothecary recommended that you remain in bed for three days."

"That is so, ma'am, and though I believe the gentleman extended his advice with my best interests in mind, I know my own capabilities. Except for a slight discoloration on my forehead, I am my old self. 'Right as a trivet,' as my father used to say."

"Nonetheless—"

"I truly wish to see the area," she added, "and since I have only the weekend remaining before I must return to London to begin rehearsals at The Haymarket Theater, for me the trip to Cromer Ridge must be tomorrow or never."

If the surprised look on Mrs. Montford's face was anything to go by, she had forgotten about Isobel's need to return to London on Monday. "Surely you can write to the manager, or whoever is in charge of the theater, and tell him you will be delayed a week or so. Explain to him about your accident. I am persuaded he will understand.''

Isobel could not resist the urge to laugh. "To the contrary, ma'am. I cannot think the man would be the least bit understanding, for theater managers are a surprisingly unsympathetic group. If I know aught of the matter, the manager, upon receiving such a letter from me, would tear my contract into a thousand pieces then lose no time in hiring another actress to play Columbine.''

"Is there nothing I can say," her hostess asked, regret in her voice, "that would influence you to stay?''

Isobel shook her head, letting the action speak for her. Speech at that moment was out of the question, for her throat had grown painfully tight. If circumstances were different, she would happily write to the theater manager on the instant, instructing him to forget he had ever heard of Isobel Townsend. Acting, even at a prestigious theater like The Haymarket, was merely the way she earned her living. For her, being on the stage could not compare to having a home and family.

If given the choice, Isobel would have rather stayed in Norfolk and been with Robert. If she were not an actress, and he were not a gentleman of wealth and social connection, nothing in the world could have dissuaded her from spending her life with him—with the man she loved—that is, if the man loved her in return.

If. If. If. Such a small word. Yet so important.

Realizing how fruitless this line of thinking was,

Isobel admonished herself for wasting these few remaining hours pining over what could never be. If she wished to make the most of the time she had left with Robert, she must put all foolish dreams from her mind, beginning that very moment. She could do that. She *would* do that.

Having made that resolve, Isobel surprised herself by asking her hostess if she might join them all later for tea.

It was a credit to Agatha Montford's sense of hospitality that she did even blink at the request. "Of course you may come down, my dear, if you are certain you feel up to it. I will have Kendrick set a place for you at table."

"No, no. Please do not, ma'am. I would not dream of putting your table out of balance. Besides, I could not possibly be dressed in time for dinner. I merely wished to make an appearance at the party—to stay no more than a few minutes—just long enough to show my respect for Lady Baysworth and to drink a toast to Lieutenant Baysworth's miraculous return."

Her statement was no more than the truth, but Isobel neglected to mention the fact that in joining the party she would improve her chances of seeing Robert, as well.

As it transpired, she spent no more than eight or ten minutes in his company, for when she joined the ladies in the music room, with its maroon and silver decor, the gentlemen still lingered over their port. Having met the vicar's wife and his sister at St. Anne's the Sunday before, Isobel curtsied to the middle-aged ladies. Then she allowed Agatha Montford to take her by the hand to introduce her to the other two ladies who made up the feminine half of the party.

It was not to be wondered at that the ladies were excited about the return of Lieutenant Gordon Baysworth, nor was it surprising that The 52nd and the battle of Corruna were acceptable topics of conversation. Isobel listened respectfully to comments made directly to her, saying all that was proper in response. Otherwise, she gave half her attention to the conversation around her and the other half to watching the door.

As luck would have it, when the gentlemen finally joined the ladies Robert was deep in conversation with the vicar, and followed that gentleman to the settee on the opposite side of the room. She dared not look at Robert overlong, lest someone guess at her feelings for him, but she knew the exact moment when he realized she was in the room. She could actually feel his gaze as it lit upon her—feel it as surely as she would have felt his hand caress her face.

She knew she need not be ashamed of her looks, for she had taken special pains with her appearance, combing a fringe of wispy curls across her forehead to hide the bruise. Tonight, in addition to the cream sarcenet dinner dress, Isobel had tied a cream-colored velvet ribbon around her neck and affixed to the ribbon the little enamel brooch that had belonged to her mother. The cleverly interlocked masks of comedy and tragedy did not show up well on the light velvet, but wearing the pin made Isobel feel as if a part of her mother went with her to the party.

When she finally allowed herself to look across the

room, Isobel's gaze went directly to Robert's—seeking, begging, for some sign that he was as happy to see her as she was to be in company with him. His brown eyes revealed nothing of what he was thinking, and if he experienced anything more than surprise at seeing her he kept that information to himself.

Isobel knew that as host Robert could not desert his dinner guests to come across the room to speak to her, but when she considered her own rapidly beating heart, his apparent calm seemed almost a slap in the face.

"Friends," Agatha Montford said, gaining her guests' attention and then indicating the footmen who were even now circling the room, carrying trays of crystal wineglasses filled with champagne, "please join me in a toast." When everyone had a glass she raised her own, saying, "To the safe return of Lieutenant Gordon Baysworth, and to the continued happiness of his mother, my dearest friend, Edith Cochran Baysworth."

Shouts of "Hear, hear!" were heard around the room, and once the toasts were drunk their hostess turned to Cecil Wolcott, asking him if he would honor them with a song. Upon seeing the way the lady's hazel eyes shone when she made her request, a casual observer might have been forgiven for attributing that sparkle to the French wine. Somehow, though, Isobel doubted that explanation.

Whatever the origin of the happy glow, the gentleman responded to the lady's request without hesitation, and within a matter of moments he was performing an appropriate, if rather sentimental, rendition of *The Soldier Boy's Return*.

The applause following the song was enthusiastic, with words of congratulation offered to the performer, and when he refused to favor them with a second selection, the vicar turned to Isobel and asked if she would give them the pleasure of hearing her.

"We saw you in Gresham two weeks ago," he said, "and were captivated by your performance as Columbine. Will you sing for us on this happy occasion?"

"Please do, my dear," Lady Baysworth said, "for we should all like to hear you."

Unable to refuse without appearing churlish, Isobel took her place at the pianoforte. She played a series of arpeggio to flex her fingers. Then, once the final chord had faded into oblivion, she began to play in earnest.

Robert watched her in silence. When he had first entered the music room, he had been surprised to discover Isobel among the ladies. She should have remained in her bed, for she needed time to recuperate from the injury inflicted upon her. Seeing her now, however, it was difficult to take issue with her being in the company, especially when she looked positively magnificent.

The modest dinner dress could not hide the slender curves of her figure, and though her hair was arranged simply, with a charming array of curls brushing her forehead, she was easily the most beautiful woman he had ever seen. And the most desirable.

Telling himself this was no time to be recalling how delectable she had felt in his arms, or the way she had responded to his kiss, nearly driving him mad with the longing to kiss her again, as she deserved to be kissed, Robert forced himself to pay attention to her performance.

Her talent upon the pianoforte was more than competent. Once she began to sing, however, none of the guests even noticed her playing, for there was something about Isobel Townsend's singing that absolutely captivated people. Hers was not the strongest voice Robert had ever heard, and it was certainly not the most dramatic, but the purity of it, the clear, uncomplicated sweetness of the tones, was bewitching.

As Robert listened to her he was reminded of the evening he had first met her, and of the moment he had stood spellbound, watching her perform the role of Columbine. In the time needed to sing one song, she had mesmerized him, making him fancy it was to him she sang, that it was him she loved. Now she was casting a similar spell upon the ladies and gentlemen gathered in his music room, and only when she finished her song and rose from the instrument was the spell broken.

A sudden, enthusiastic burst of applause broke the silence that followed, and the other guests—all save one—rushed forward to congratulate Isobel upon her talent. Only one person remained in his seat, and that one was Cecil Wolcott.

Isobel loved to sing, and though it was part of the way in which she earned her livelihood, she still enjoyed knowing that others had been moved by her music. A few compliments, sincerely extended, were always welcome, but she found too much attention just a bit embarrassing. For that reason, she was pleased when the vicar's sister was asked to recite one of her poems; it forced everyone to return to their places and allowed Isobel to move to the other side of the room. To her surprise, she was joined there only moments later by Mr. Cecil Wolcott, who pulled a slipper chair quite close to Isobel's.

"It would appear," he began quietly, speaking low enough not to disturb the poetry recitation, "that you are a young woman of many talents."

Not for a minute was Isobel fooled into thinking his words a compliment. Actually, from the cold, expressionless look in his eyes, the comment might have been an insult. Before she had time to consider the matter, Mr. Wolcott continued.

"I hope you are not too disappointed that Lieutenant Baysworth has been heard from."

"Disappointed? Sir, I am elated for her ladyship. Anyone who knows her must rejoice at the return of her son."

"Almost anyone," he corrected. "You, for one, might be forgiven for being less inclined to celebrate. Especially since this wonderful news reduces her ladyship's need for a niece."

Isobel stiffened, but though she was affronted by such an accusation she did not wish to make a scene and ruin the party. "I should think, sir, that not even a real niece could possibly fill the place of a beloved child."

"I would not know," he said. "My brother was never blessed with children. Therefore, I have neither niece, nephew, nor child." The remark was innocuous enough, but with Cecil Wolcott watching her every reaction, Isobel doubted that anything he said or did was without some ulterior motive.

" 'Tis a pity," she said, "for you might have found the experience of being an uncle enriching."

"Perhaps," he said, his tone cold, "unless the child's only purpose in claiming kinship was to enrich himself, or herself, at my and my brother's expense."

"From your words, sir, one might almost think such a thing had already happened."

The gentleman muttered something beneath his breath, and though Isobel did not hear the words she knew instinctively that she would not find them to her liking. "Young woman," he said, "why do you not abandon this charade and be done with it?"

"What charade is that, sir? I assure you, I have no idea to what you refer."

"You are a consummate actress—I will give you that. But whatever your plans—whatever your ill-conceived schemes—they will not succeed. Allow me to be frank, Miss Townsend. You are not talented enough to extort money from the Wolcott estate."

"Extort money! Are you mad, sir? A week ago I did not even know that you, or your brother, existed."

He sighed, as if his patience was at an end. "I see you intend to play this farce to its conclusion."

"You *are* mad."

"You may call me so, Miss Townsend, if it makes you feel better, but I warn you: do not make the mistake of thinking me a fool."

Isobel bit back a rather scathing estimate of his intelligence, for some remaining shred of good manners compelled her to keep that opinion to herself. Still, she had not been self-supporting for five years without learning how to stand up for herself. "Since you have chosen to speak frankly, Mr. Wolcott, I believe I should be afforded the same courtesy."

"Speak, by all means, young woman. And if any truth be in you, pray let it be spoken now."

"You do not like me, sir, and almost from the moment you arrived at Montford House you have made little effort to conceal your feelings. At least, you have chosen not to conceal your dislike from me. How you explain your behavior to our hostess and Lady Baysworth, I do not know, but—"

"I wondered when her ladyship's name would come into this conversation."

Isobel felt as though she were trying to reason with a lunatic. "Lady Baysworth's name was mentioned scarce two minutes ago, sir. And even if that had not been so, what difference can that make to you?"

Over his handsome face, Cecil Wolcott wore an invisible mask. That mask was slipping now, revealing the man's anger. "The difference, as you well know, is that her ladyship is a wealthy woman, and until today she was a wealthy woman without kith or kin. Now, of course, her son is miraculously returned to her, and she will have little need for a fraudulent niece."

The mask slipped entirely, and the look he gave her was filled with abhorrence. "You will be obliged, I think, Miss Townsend, to find some other sheep to shear. Be warned, however, that it will not be I."

"You! What makes you suppose that I would—"

"Stay away from me," he said, the words spoken from between straight, angry lips. "Stay away from my brother. And stay away from Wolcott Park. Be advised, we have no tolerance for fraudulent relatives."

Before Isobel could respond, he leaned very close to her, his face mere inches from her own. "If you should try to extort money from us, madam, either now or at any time in the future, rest assured that I will bring suit against you."

"Mr. Wolcott, whatever it is you think you know of me, allow me to inform you that—"

"No, madam, allow *me* to do the informing. I have already consulted a solicitor who has tried and won many such cases, and though Sir Anthony advised me to ignore you altogether, I could not do that. As soon as the Bow Street Runner approached me, I knew I could not remain passive. I am a man of action, Miss Townsend, and I wished to see my enemy face-to-face."

He glared at her, his gray eyes hard, implacable. "Be advised, young woman, that under no circumstances will you ever be heir to Wolcott Park."

This entire conversation bordered on lunacy, and Isobel wished she had never allowed herself to be cornered by Cecil Wolcott. *Lawyers? Suits? Bow Street Runners?* What did any of those things have to do with her?

"Mr. Wolcott," she said, striving to be the voice of reason in a situation that was completely irrational, "if someone has threatened you with legal action you have my sympathy, but you must believe me when I tell you that I am not that person. I do not now, nor have I ever, represented myself to be heir to your estate."

"And yet," he said, "you would have the world

believe that you are the legitimate daughter of Fiona Cochran and Byron Smyth."

So that was what this bizarre conversation was all about. Would no one believe her that she was not Fiona's daughter?

"I have told Lady Baysworth repeatedly that I am not her niece, and on more than one occasion I have even told *you* that I am not her niece."

"Yes, you have, and it is a clever ruse. But not clever enough, for I see through your scheme."

Exasperated, Isobel said, "I am the daughter of Mary and Thomas Townsend. I had hoped that my word would be enough to satisfy any interested party, but apparently I was mistaken. Since you will not let the subject rest, I must resort to rudeness and demand to know what business it is of yours whose child I am."

Quite angry by now, Isobel added, "Even if I were the result of the union between Fiona Cochran and the actor, Byron Smyth, I cannot understand what possible concern that would be of yours."

"It would concern me greatly, madam, for *I* am Byron Smyth!"

Twelve

From the moment Cecil Wolcott approached Isobel, Robert had found an unobtrusive spot in the corner of the music room from where he could observe the pair, his purpose to be at hand should the lady have need of him. He still had no firm idea which of the two suspects had attacked Isobel at the brook. A dozen men had been searching for Willem Potter since afternoon with no success. If Potter should prove innocent of the crime, that left Wolcott as the prime suspect.

Robert could not hear what was being said, but judging by the unsmiling look on Isobel's face she and Wolcott were not discussing the latest song titles. Therefore, when Isobel's posture became ramrod straight, giving evidence of her increasing vexation, Robert decided it was time he made his way toward her.

He reached her chair just in time to hear Wolcott's revelation that *he* was Byron Smyth.

Disguising his surprise, and smiling at the pair in a manner that would not raise the curiosity of the other guests, Robert leaned close and spoke quietly. "Come with me, both of you. This conversation should be continued in private."

"Sir," Wolcott began, "this is none of your concern, and I—"

Robert stopped him with one long, hard look, a look that said the suggestion of privacy was not to be ignored.

Taking Wolcott's acquiescence for granted, Robert put his hand beneath Isobel's elbow and led her from the music room, down to the end of the corridor, then into the book room. Once the door was closed behind them and Isobel had disposed herself upon one of the red leather wing chairs, Robert perched on the edge of the ornate ebony desk, his arms folded across his chest and his attention fixed upon the man who claimed to be Byron Smyth.

As for Wolcott, he chose to stand beside the fireplace, almost as if he hoped to distance himself from the proceedings. He did not look at Robert; instead, he pretended interest in the antique brass carriage clock on the mantel.

Robert waited until the man abandoned his examination of the clock before he spoke. "And now," he said, "I should like to know why you wormed your way into my home using a false name."

Wolcott gave him stare for stare. "Any falsehood to be exposed here is not of my creating. I am, as I stated from the beginning, Cecil Wolcott of Wolcott Park, in Sussex." He turned toward Isobel, distaste causing his finely chiseled nostrils to flare. "If you wish to discuss prevarication, Montford, I suggest you begin with that young woman, whoever she may be."

Robert squashed the desire to smash his fist into those flaring nostrils. "I know exactly who the young *lady* is, for she has been the soul of honesty from the very beginning of our acquaintance."

"Ha! She is an actress, sir. Make-believe is her stock and trade."

"And yet, I trust her."

"Naturally," Wolcott said, his voice filled with disdain. "You force me to speak bluntly, Montford, when I should prefer not to do so, but—"

"Please," Robert said, the scowl on his face giving the lie to his polite words, "do not feel you must spare my feelings."

"Very well. Let me say only this: beautiful women such as Miss Townsend know to a nicety how to inspire a young man to think with his passions rather than his brains."

Embarrassment burned in Isobel's cheeks at such outspokenness, and she wanted nothing so much as to get up and leave the room. This conversation had nothing to do with her, even though Cecil Wolcott had taken it into his head that she was involved in some nefarious scheme to defraud him, and she could think of no reason why she should remain to hear further insults. The man disliked her—that was obvious—and she had endured just about enough from him. She would not sit quietly while he vilified her before Robert.

If her face was warm, Robert's was icy cold; at least his eyes were. "I suggest," he said, his tone as frigid as the gaze of those brown orbs, "that you refrain from mentioning Miss Townsend again. Furthermore, if you do not wish to be thrown from this house upon the instant, you had better start explaining why you said you were Byron Smyth."

"I said I was Smyth, because I am. Or rather, I used to be."

For a moment, Isobel thought the gentleman had said all he meant to say, but he had only begun. Apparently he had decided to tell the entire story, for he walked over to the wing chair opposite hers and settled himself comfortably. "I was a second son," he began, "and because the title and Wolcott Park would one day go to my brother I needed to choose a profession. Unfortunately, I am not pious enough for the church, nor brave enough for the army."

If he meant that remark to charm them he was wide of the mark, for Isobel remained impassive and Robert continued to stare icily at him. "So you chose the stage," Robert said.

Wolcott nodded. "I possessed a pleasant singing voice, and I had a flair for recitation, so it seemed the natural choice. My family, as you may imagine, was less than pleased by my decision, so to save them from any embarrassment I took a new name."

Isobel found her interest piqued in spite of her earlier anger at the man, and she asked him if he was the same Byron Smyth who had played Hamlet twenty-five years ago at The Gresham Theater. "Are you the actor who eloped with Lady Baysworth's sister?"

At first she thought he meant to ignore her question, but after a slight hesitation he nodded. "I know that eloping was a reprehensible act, and I am not proud that I agreed to the plan, but in my own defense I was but four and twenty, and completely captivated. In the year I had been with the troupe I had grown accustomed to the adulation of the women in the audiences. One night, however, I looked beyond the footlights and there sat the most beautiful girl I had ever seen. I believe I fell in love that very instant."

"Fiona?" Isobel asked.

"Fiona," Wolcott replied. His voice had a faraway quality to it, as though he had become lost in his memories. "Fiona was only seventeen, and the pampered darling of adoring parents. She was young, she was spoiled, and her head was filled with romantic fantasies. Of course, no one was ever less suited than she to be the wife of an actor in a traveling troupe. Still, when the time came to quit Gresham and continue to the next town, Fiona professed her undying love for me, and I knew I could not leave without her."

Robert appeared unmoved by the story of young love. "So," he said, "you took Fiona from her home and from the protection of her family, without ever letting them know what became of her. Such callousness cannot be laid entirely to youth."

Wolcott had been studying his folded hands, but now he looked up. "Of that final sin, at least, you may absolve me, for I wrote to her family. I informed Sir Harold of the time and place of our marriage, and sent him my itinerary so he might write to Fiona. He never answered my letter. Also, when I received word of Fiona's death, I wrote to him as soon as I was able. Again, I received no reply."

Isobel felt a tug at her heart for the young girl whose father had turned his back on her. Fiona, petted as she had been all her life, must have been devastated by her father's silence.

"*Received word?*" Robert said, apparently more interested in the latter part of the man's statement.

"Are we to understand that you were not with Fiona at the time of her demise?"

When Cecil Wolcott replied, his voice was husky, as if with remembered grief. "In the ten months we had been married, Fiona had grown weary of the traveling. Even when we arrived in London. Town seemed to hold no interest for her. She was not feeling well, and she spoke constantly of settling down. She missed having a home and the stability it provided. As well, she was jealous of the many women who thought themselves enamored of me. We fought constantly as a result of her jealousy, and after one particularly heated argument Fiona just disappeared."

Isobel gasped, for she knew how inhospitable the city could be.

Robert was equally aghast. "She disappeared in London? And you never found her?" His tone became accusatory. "Did you try?"

"Of course I tried!"

Agitated, the gentleman ran his fingers through his hair, upsetting the thick, gray-sprinkled blond locks. "We may have argued, but Fiona was still my wife, and I loved her. I searched for days, nearly beside myself with worry, until one of the women in the troupe finally took pity on me and told me Fiona had been seen getting into a hired coach with one of the actors from the troupe. The man had always been solicitous of Fiona's comfort, but he was a shy fellow, rather reserved, and I had never thought him a threat to my marriage.

"The word around the theater was that he had decided to give up the stage and return to his home. Apparently, Fiona had decided to go with him."

"But you could not know that for certain," Robert

said. "Be that as it may, you now had a clue. Did you follow them to the fellow's home?"

"I could not. Like me, the man had adopted a professional name, and I had no idea what his real name might be. Furthermore, with him being such a quiet, unassuming sort of fellow, no one in the company had ever paid enough attention to him to remember where he said he lived. Somewhere in the south of England was all anyone knew."

Isobel believed him. Actors were a varied lot, and though most were outgoing and discussed themselves and their interests at every opportunity, it was not unusual for one or two among them to be rather quiet, with none of the other actors paying them much attention. Her own dear, kind father must have been just such a one, for Thomas Townsend was a private man, one who listened with a sympathetic ear to the troubles of others but kept his own counsel.

"I would have persevered in my search in any case," Mr. Wolcott continued, "had I not succumbed to the influenza. You will not remember, I am sure, but the epidemic of that winter was particularly virulent, and thousands died as a result of the rapid spread of the disease throughout the country. I would have been among that number had it not been for the fortunate circumstance of my brother's being in Town and looking me up."

Isobel could not stop her impetuous question. "Your family had not severed all ties with you, then?"

"No. At least not my brother, for he is the kindest and best of men. I remember none of what happened, you understand, but my brother found me as near death as one may be and still have a chance at survival. Hoping to save my life, he whisked me home to Wolcott Park, where he saw that I was given the best of care. Even so, I was ill for the better part of ten months.

"I had only just begun to regain my health when I received a letter that had been sent in care of the manager of the acting troupe a month earlier. It had been misdirected, but it finally reached my home. In that letter, the man I knew only by his stage name wrote to tell me that Fiona was dead. She, too, had fallen prey to the influenza. She died, the fellow was good enough to inform me, with my name upon her lips. She asked him to tell me that she was sorry she had left me, and that she loved me still."

He paused to clear his throat. "As I said earlier, I wrote to Sir Harold and Lady Cochran informing them of their daughter's demise. They never responded. I sincerely regret that Sir Harold's pride kept him from telling his other daughter about Fiona. I consider that an unconscionable piece of arrogance."

Isobel readily agreed with the assessment. "And after your illness, you never returned to the stage?"

Wolcott looked at her as if surprised to discover that she was still in the room. "After my recuperation I remained at Wolcott Park. With Fiona lost to me, I had no more heart for the theater."

"It is a sad story," Isobel said, "and I can readily understand how you must have felt when you heard that your wife—"

"Please, young woman, keep your sympathies for those who are foolish enough to trust in their sincerity. I renounced the acting life because I wanted nothing more to do with the theater or with anyone connected with it. And I want nothing to do with you." He gave her a look that was filled with loathing. "I hope I make myself clear."

After listening to Wolcott's story, Isobel had felt sincere compassion for him. Now, of course, she felt only embarrassment, for the man still despised her. "Sir, you make yourself perfectly clear, and I—"

"Robert?" Agatha Montford called, opening the door slightly. "Are you in there?" Since she followed her question by stepping inside the book room, no reply was necessary. "The vicar and his ladies are leaving, and they wish to take their leave of you. What in heaven's name induced you to abandon our guests, I cannot even imagine. Your absence was remarked, and Edith and I—"

She stopped short, for she had just noticed the presence of Isobel and that of Cecil Wolcott, whose hair was noticeably mussed. "Cecil," she said, going directly to him, her hands outstretched, "what is amiss?"

The gentleman stood at her entrance and took her hands in his, holding them with such ease that an observer might be forgiven for thinking that he had held them numerous times before. "I told your son my true identity," he said. "As I had feared, he was censorious of my behavior. Not that I blame him, of course, for I would give ten years of my life if I could reshape the past."

The lady squeezed his hands, offering him comfort. "What is done cannot be undone. We have both lived long enough to know that."

Isobel watched the exchange. Then she looked toward the desk to see how Robert had reacted. His face showed nothing of his thoughts, and if he was bothered by seeing his mother offer comfort to a man he had reason to distrust, he chose not to reveal it at present."Come," he said, rising from the desk and offering his arm to Isobel. "Walk with me to say good-bye to the vicar. Then I will escort you to your bedchamber. I am persuaded you should have been abed long ago."

Having no wish to remain in company with a man who despised her for no reason, Isobel rose from the red leather wing chair.

As she crossed to the door, she thought she stepped on some small object that had fallen to the carpet, but she was too eager to quit the room to stop to see what it was.

As she preceded Robert from the book room, he turned back to look at Cecil Wolcott. "I will return, sir, for our conversation is not finished. There is much more I wish to know."

The man said nothing, for his attention was caught by the ribbon that had been tied around Isobel Townsend's neck; the ribbon now lay on the carpet, and he stared fixedly at the little enamel brooch attached to the strip of silk. Slowly, as if he could not believe the testimony of his eyes, he bent to retrieve the trinket, his gaze never leaving the two delicate, interlocked masks, the one smiling, the other wearing a frown.

"Oh, dear," Mrs. Montford said, "Isobel has dropped her brooch. Here," she said, holding out her hand, "I will take it to her, for I know she sets great store by it. It belonged to her mother."

"No," he said, the word barely audible, "it cannot be true."

"Of course it is. Isobel told me how her father gave her the brooch when she went off to school. I believe his words were, 'To help you remember a beautiful lady who died much too young."

While Cecil Wolcott stared at the interlocked masks of comedy and tragedy, his lips began to tremble. He caught his lower lip between his teeth to still its quivering. Then, as if to disprove what his every feeling told him was true, he closed his eyes and ran his forefinger around the thin filigree that joined the two masks. He gasped as he discovered the skillfully hidden initials, one an F, the other a C.

"What is it?" Mrs. Montford asked

"Fiona," he whispered. "This belonged to Fiona."

After a silence broken only by the ticking of the brass carriage clock on the mantel, Cecil Wolcott opened his eyes and looked at the brooch once more. "I had it made for my bride to commemorate her eighteenth birthday. It was not a very expensive trinket, for we lived on my actor's wages and I could not afford anything nicer. But Fiona loved it. She wore it all the time, and she always said she would one day pass it on to her daughter. *Our daughter.*"

As if only just realizing what this meant, he held his breath, too awed by the knowledge to do more than whisper the words. "When last I saw Fiona, she had been feeling poorly. I thought it was a cold coming on. Foolish me, I never even suspected she might be with child."

Then he groaned, and it was the sound of one who fears he has burned his bridges. "Isobel Townsend is Fiona's daughter. My daughter. And she probably hates me." He hid his face in his hands. "Heaven help me," he muttered. "What have I done!"

Thirteen

Robert had not wanted to take Isobel to Cromer Ridge, and only after she had sworn that she was perfectly well and that her head no longer gave her even the slightest discomfort did he relent.

"We will discuss it again in the morning," he said, stopping just outside the door to her bedchamber. "If you sleep well tonight and awake refreshed, I will have the phaeton brought around as soon as you have broken your fast."

"Tomorrow," she had said, seeing no point in discussion, "at eight of the clock, I will meet you belowstairs in the vestibule—rested, fed, and ready to go."

His only response was a smile. Then, as if he could not stop himself, he reached out and ran the tip of his finger along her jaw, pausing just beneath her chin. Isobel thought he meant to turn her face up for a kiss, and though she had sworn never to see him again once she left Montford House she had made no such promise about allowing him to kiss her while she was still with him. To her disappointment, he had merely stared at her lips before stepping back and making her a rather formal bow. "Until tomorrow," he said, "but only if you are well."

"I will be."

Isobel watched him turn and retrace his steps to the stairs, then entered her room and prepared herself for bed. She had been so happy to know she would have all of the next day alone with Robert that she would have crawled from a sickbed if it had been necessary.

As it turned out, such a sacrifice was not required of her, for she awoke feeling quite like her old self. After eating the toast and hot chocolate Meg brought her, Isobel donned her walking boots, a serviceable, dark blue frock, and the coverall apron Robert had insisted she would need for the dig. Then she grabbed her chip straw bonnet and hurried from the room.

As arranged, Robert waited in the vestibule, and as he caught sight of her in one of Meg's aprons, a smile pulled at the corners of his mouth. "Since you have come dressed for a dig, madam, I suppose it would be fruitless to suggest that we merely go for a stroll in the rose garden."

"You may suggest it, sir, but be advised that I will look upon anything short of the promised trip to Cromer Ridge as a poor substitute. I assure you, I feel perfectly healthy, and quite eager to observe that mysterious *something* you promised to show me. You said it was fascinating, and a sight I would not forget as long as I lived."

As if making one last attempt to dissuade her, Robert said, "But what of the dangers of climbing up the mountain? When we discussed it before, you had your doubts about the outing, listing among your reservations your inability to fly. Never tell me you have learned how since that day."

"Make sport of me if you must, sir, but even

though I have not that talent you describe I refuse
to be gainsaid. You pledged to show me something
older than man. Older, or so you said, than most of
the animals that now roam the earth. Now you find
me positively agog to discover what that thing may
be."

"Very well, madam, if it is a dig you wish, a dig
you will have."

Isobel could tell from the lightness in Robert's
voice that he was not displeased she had insisted
upon the trip to the ridge, and without further ado
he led her out to the front portico, where a groom
stood at the heads of the team. The grays were as
eager to be on their way as were the two humans,
and within a matter of minutes Isobel and Robert
were seated in the phaeton, the *clop, clop* of the
horses' hooves sounding on the crushed rock carriageway.

As the phaeton passed between the brick columns
that supported the wrought iron entrance gates, Isobel made up her mind that she would entertain
no thoughts that would hinder her enjoyment of the
day. That crazy old poacher Willem Potter was banished from her memory, as was Cecil Wolcott, a man
who disliked her for no apparent reason. Though
she knew her heart would ache for Robert once she
returned to London, she would leave that melan-
choly prospect in the future, where it belonged. For
now, she gave herself over to the joy of spending
this one last day with the man she loved.

It was a glorious morning, with the soft, musical
song of meadow pipits filling the air, and as the
phaeton sped in a northeasterly direction, Isobel was
impressed by the change in topography. Within a

short span of time they had progressed from gentle, undramatic landscape to wooded slopes and heights that produced unexpected and impressive scenery, and as they approached the ridge, Isobel noticed an increase in heather and bracken, sure signs of sandy, gravelly land ahead.

Within minutes, Robert turned the team toward a small meadow that had been roped off by a pair of men who were father and son—if their flaming orange hair and freckled faces were anything to judge by. At sight of the phaeton, the younger of the men came at a run to take charge of the horses.

After tossing the fellow a coin, Robert informed Isobel that Cromer Ridge was a moraine. "A moraine left by the glaciers of eons past," he added. Having offered her that tidbit, he climbed down from the phaeton and turned back to her, holding up his arms to help her alight. "What I wish to show you, however, is just beyond the cliffs, at their base, in the peaty beds which are believed to have been formed during a warm, interglacial period."

Isobel did not move from where she sat. "Wait just a minute," she said, suddenly suspicious. "When we were at The Broads, you told me those lakes had once been peat beds, and that proof of their history was buried beneath the water. In order to see whatever it is you wished to show me here, will I find myself obliged to dig in knee-deep mud?"

Robert chuckled, the sound deep in his chest and immensely appealing. *"Now* you ask that question."

As if he had every right to do so, he reached for her, placing his hands on either side of her waist and swinging her down from the carriage, all the while giving her a teasing look that quite stole her breath away. "Your concern comes a bit late, madam, for, mud or no, to cry craven now would be unconscionable."

That teasing look, plus the wondrous feel of Robert's strong hands circling her waist, were worth any amount of mud, but Isobel refrained from telling him so. Instead, she said, "Unconscionable or not, I should like to know if I am destined to return to Montford House covered in goo."

"Only if you fall in," he replied, his mouth twitching with the effort not to laugh.

"That makes me feel *much* more confident."

While he laughed, Isobel said, "If I may be so bold as to ask, what are my chances of taking a tumble into the bog?"

"That all depends on how close you stay to me."

Isobel saw no difficulty in that, for she was more than willing to stay close to him, as close as he would allow.

As they talked, they had been walking steadily uphill, and as the terrain grew rockier Robert took her hand to assist her. "Do not worry," he said, giving her hand a squeeze. "I promise to keep you from harm's way."

They continued for perhaps fifteen minutes, with the climb becoming increasingly more steep, and—just as Isobel decided she could not continue—they crested the chalky cliff. The view was not at all what she had expected, and as her gaze followed the path of the clear blue waterfall that all but obscured the mud-covered peat beds below, she breathed an awed sigh. "It is like a scene from my childhood history lessons. One can readily imagine this spot looking exactly this way when mastodons roamed the earth."

"You are not far off the mark," Robert said, pointing to the wide expanse of thick, brown mire. "Down there scientists and amateurs alike have found the remains of all manner of prehistoric animals. Elephant, bear, hippopotamus, rhinoceros, even saber-toothed tigers."

When he spoke, his voice was filled with that same excitement Isobel had heard when he told her of the paleo-scientists who dug in the soggy earth below The Broads. While she listened to his words, it occurred to her how unfortunate it was that he had been obliged to run the Montford estate and could not pursue the scientific work he loved.

"You told me that your boyhood finds were mostly fossilized insects, and fragments of bones you hoped were those of the dinosaurs. Have you visited the ridge since you became an adult? And if so, have you found anything more significant than bugs?"

He nodded. "Yes, to both questions. But come, let me show you what I promised."

He took her hand again and led her around a ledge perhaps eight feet wide. Though the path was more than adequate for safe walking, it serpentined, following the ins and outs of the cliff face. For that reason, Isobel moved slowly and cautiously, never once letting go of Robert's hand. When he finally stopped, he remained quiet, gazing at the chalk wall but saying nothing, allowing her to discover the treasure for herself.

At first Isobel saw only the gray-white earth, with a bit of bracken appearing here and there. Then, as she paid closer attention, she began to notice ripples in the ridge face. In time those ripples began to take shape, and as she touched them with her

finger, slowly tracing the outlines, she became excited about what lay beneath the surface. "Robert,"
she whispered, "are those bones?"

"You have a good eye. For they are, indeed, bones,
and not from just any old animal. I am convinced
that is the foot of a dinosaur. See here," he said,
removing a small pick from his pocket and scraping
away at a bit of the chalk. "I believe that is part of
the metatarsus, the hind foot in a quadruped."

"How very exciting," she said. "Why have you
never dug it out so you might examine it more
closely?"

Robert did not reply right away. Instead, he
searched her eyes, as if he had a question of his
own—an important question, one that needed an
answer. He must have found what he sought, for he
smiled at her, and the look he gave her was so sweet,
so gentle, she found it difficult to breathe. "The
reason I did not dig it out before, though I was unaware of my motives at the time, was because I was
waiting for you."

After reaching inside his coat once again, he withdrew a small hand axe and a housepainter's brush.
Giving the brush to her, he said, "Use small, careful
strokes. This job requires patience."

They had been working together for the better
part of an hour, with Robert carefully chipping away
at the chalk face and Isobel gently brushing aside
the scrapings, when Isobel heard someone moving
rather cautiously along the path. Assuming it was
another amateur paleo-scientist, curious to see what
they were doing, she turned to watch the newcomer's approach.

To Isobel's surprise, the scruffy little man who

rounded the corner was known to her; he was the poacher she had met at the brook. Astounded to see him there, she gasped.

At the sound of her indrawn breath, Robert looked up. "Potter!" he said. "What the devil are you doing here?"

"Well, now," Willem Potter replied, "I'm a curious fellow, I am, and I wanted to see for myself what was so all fired interesting that you would order the phaeton brought around so you could bring miss there up to Cromer Ridge."

Robert was not deceived by Potter's claim of curiosity. If the devious little man had followed them all the way to the ridge it was for reasons of his own, and Robert knew enough of Willem Potter to distrust those reasons. Furthermore, the man's right hand was behind his back, and as he spoke he slid his other hand into the pocket of his filthy smock.

The action, slow though it was, put Robert on guard, and he put his arm around Isobel's waist and began edging his way around her so that he would be between her and Potter. Hoping to distract the fellow, Robert asked him how he knew they were coming to the ridge.

"I heard the grooms talking." He grinned, as if delighted to reveal the fact that he had been on the property undetected. "Since yesterday, I been hiding out in the loft of your stables."

Biting back an oath, Robert assumed a calm he did not feel. "How clever of you."

Potter did not take the remark as a compliment. "What else was I to do? With you setting men on my trail like I was vermin to be hunted down, I couldn't stay at my cottage, so I hid out in the one place I knew no one would think to look. After you drove off in that fancy phaeton, I stole one of the farm horses and followed you."

"But why would you do that? Follow us, I mean."

"Why?" He all but snarled, and the lifting of his lip gave his loutish face a decidedly feral look. "I'm here 'cause I got me a score to settle."

Having said this, Potter looked directly at Isobel, and as he stared at her he moved his right arm, revealing a slingshot, the kind many of the tenants carried. At the same time, he withdrew his other hand from the pocket of his smock. In his grimy palm lay a stone about the size of a plum.

"I reckon I got you to thank for my present troubles, missy. Too bad I didn't silence you when I had the chance. Guess my aim was off a bit that other time, but I'm closer now."

He put the rock in the slingshot and moved as if to take aim. "This time I won't miss."

"Wait!" Robert shouted. "It was not Miss Townsend who sent the men looking for you. That was my doing. If you have an argument with anyone, it is with me."

"Could be I got reason to dislike you both." He laughed then, but the sound held no humor. "By the way, how did you like them mushrooms I left at the kitchen door?"

Before Robert could reply, Potter said, "I got plenty of rocks here in my pocket. More than enough to stone the two of you."

Robert's blood ran cold. He was not afraid for himself, for he knew he could overpower Willem Potter if the coward would just come a few feet closer, but when he thought about harm possibly coming to Isobel, his insides knotted with fear. If he tried to rush Potter, Isobel would be left unprotected, exposed to the villain's aim, and the vengeful little man had vowed he would not miss, not this time.

Even if the blow did no more than glance off her forehead as his previous one had and merely knocked her unconscious, the path on which they stood offered little room for missteps. If she lost her footing, there was a chance she might fall over the side of the cliff, where certain death awaited.

"Why not let the lady go?" Robert said. "Once she is gone you and I can discuss the problem, man to man, as it were."

Potter shook his head. "She stays. And there'll be no discussing, as you call it. I'm through taking orders from high-and-mighty toffs like you who think they've a right to lord it over a fellow. From now on, things'll be done like *I* say. Me. Willem Potter."

Obviously considering the matter settled, Potter adjusted the rock in the leather and pulled the sling taut, as if to test its readiness. "I mean to stone you first, Montford, 'cause I want missy there to see you pitch over the side of the cliff."

Isobel gasped, and the little man laughed. "It'll be worth the ride here just to watch her face when she hears you land in that slime pit below. She's in love with you. I can tell that from the fear in her eyes—fear I didn't see when it was just her and me on the bridge the other day—and making her watch you die will be like killing her twice."

The man was clearly deranged, but if Robert could keep him talking long enough he might convince him to let Isobel go. "You are mistaken," he said,

forcing a smile to his lips in hopes of appearing disinterested. "The lady does not care for me at all.
You have but to ask her."

"She'll lie," Potter said. "Females are born liars,
every one of them."

"Not Miss Townsend. She *always* tells the truth."
Robert turned his head slightly, so that he might
speak over his shoulder. "Tell him, Isobel. Tell him
you do not love me."

When Isobel remained silent, Robert muttered beneath his breath. "Isobel! For the love of heaven,
do as I say. This may be your only hope of escape.
Tell him you do not love me."

"Well," Willem Potter said, "speak up, missy. Tell
me the truth, and if your answer's 'no,' mayhap I'll
let you go. Do you love him, or don't you?"

Robert held his breath, willing her to say the
words that would save her.

"I do love him," she said. "I love him with all my
heart."

Fourteen

I love him with all my heart. Robert could not believe Isobel had said those words, for by doing so she had signed her own death warrant.

Why could she not have lied, just this once?

Feeling more desperate by the moment, he was trying to think what he could do to save the situation when he heard someone on the path, just a short distance behind Potter. That someone was traveling at a run, and from the noise of his footfalls it seemed the person was no lightweight.

"What the deuce!" Potter said, turning to see who was coming up behind him. Judging by the haste with which he took several steps back, the little man was terrified to find himself suddenly face-to-face with a stranger whose broad shoulders and thick neck resembled those of an ox. As for the newcomer, he stopped short, not even breathing hard.

"What 'ave we 'ere?" Jethro Comstock asked, looking from Potter to Robert, then returning his attention to the slingshot Potter held. "Appears to be a bit of a to-do."

From the pinched expression on Potter's face, he was waging an inner battle between frustration and fear, but he attempted to bluff his way through

"Whoever you are, this don't concern you, so turn around and go back where you came from."

The Bow Street Runner ignored the directive and made himself comfortable by leaning his massive shoulder against the chalky cliff face. Moving slowly, as if he had all the time in the world, he removed a silver toothpick from his waistcoat pocket and placed the item between his fleshy lips. "Use your *nous* box, little man," he said quietly. "Drop the slingshot and give over peaceful like, and I won't 'ave no cause to 'urt you."

The softly spoken threat was more than enough to frighten a weasel like Potter, but when the oversized fellow straightened and took one step forward, the smaller man panicked. His face contorted with fear. Potter stepped back, and then he turned to run. In his haste to put distance between him and Comstock, he forgot the need for caution on the narrow path, and he stepped on the patch of loose chalk Isobel had brushed away from the imbedded dinosaur bones.

Potter's thick-soled boots skidded on the scree, and though he waved his arms fiercely it was no use—he could not maintain his balance.

Instinctively, Robert rushed forward to pull the scraggly little man back from harm's way. The misadventure would have ended there and all would have been well, had Potter not fought his rescuer. Apparently he believed that Robert meant to push him over the edge.

"No!" he screamed, and the cry seemed to echo up and down the mountain.

Isobel watched in horror, her heart clamoring against her ribs, as the men struggled. Finally, Potter caught at the lapels of Robert's coat, clutching at the material with a strength multiplied by fear. Robert dug in his heels, and for a moment Isobel thought he had prevailed. Unfortunately, ill luck was with him, and when he took one step back it was onto the loose chalk. As if doomed from the start, both men pitched over the side of the cliff.

They fell silently. No screams, no curses. One minute they were there, struggling; the next they disappeared over the edge.

Isobel stood as if turned to stone, while an eerie stillness seemed to hang about the place—a stillness that even the rush of the waterfall could not dispel.

Into that ominous quiet came Cecil Wolcott, his breath coming in great gasps as if he had run all the way up the mountain. "Isobel," he said, stopping beside the large man, "are you all right?"

She did not answer. She could not, for her brain would allow only one coherent thought. *Robert is not dead! Robert is not dead!*

She had seen him go over the cliff; yet something inside her refused to believe the testimony of her eyes.

Cecil Wolcott approached her and slipped his arm around her shoulders. "Come," he said, his tone gentle, caring, "let me take you back to my carriage. Comstock will do what is necessary here. You have received a shock, and should—"

"No," she said, pulling out of the circle of his arm. "I cannot leave Robert here alone."

With that, she dropped to her knees and crawled to the edge of the cliff. "Robert," she called, raising her voice to be heard above the sound of the falling water. "Can you hear me?"

Wolcott was beside her once again. "My dear girl, you must come away. This is a terrible tragedy, but you cannot change what has happened. Why do you not allow me to—"

"Be quiet!" she said. "I cannot hear."

"But, my dear, there is nothing to hear. Robert cannot possibly have survived such a fall, and—"

"Robert!" she yelled again, ignoring the man beside her. "Robert, can you hear me?"

"Isobel," came a faint call from somewhere below. "Robert!"

Feeling as if her heart had begun to beat again after a painful cessation, Isobel lay flat on her stomach and inched as close as possible to the chalky edge, hanging her head over so she could see the cliff face. "Robert. I cannot see you. Where are you?"

"On a ledge," he answered, "perhaps twenty feet down."

"Are you . . . are you hurt?"

"Only a little. I dare not move, though, for the ledge is quite narrow, and it is slippery from the spray of the waterfall."

"Oh, Robert, I was so frightened. I—"

Whatever she had meant to say, she was forestalled by a pair of thick, determined hands that took hold of her feet and pulled her away from the edge.

"Up you come, miss," the ox-like man said, lifting her by the elbows and setting her on her feet. "Let me 'ave a look-see at the situation. Climbed out a few windows in my day, I 'ave, and never a scratch to show for it, so don't you worry. I'll 'ave the gentleman up in two shakes of a lamb's tail, or my name ain't Jethro Comstock."

Comstock lay on his stomach as Isobel had done, and though his inspection took slightly more than two shakes, he did not dally. "I see 'im," he said, coming carefully to his feet. "It's like the gentleman said—the ledge is a might narrow."

Isobel pressed her fingernails into her palms, hoping the pain would force her to remain calm. Robert would need all the help he could get, and she would need a clear head, if for no other reason than to act as dogsbody to the competent-looking Mr. Comstock. "Have you a plan, sir?"

"I do, but first I'll need a rope."

Isobel tried to think. She had seen rope lately. But where? Fear and frustration brought tears to her eyes, but they dried fast enough when she recalled the two men with the flaming orange hair. "The meadow where we left the phaeton and pair," she said, the words tumbling out. "The men have it roped off."

When she turned and would have bolted back down the narrow path, the big man caught her by the arm, effectively stopping her in her tracks. "I'll fetch the rope, miss."

"Yes," Wolcott agreed, taking her other arm as if he thought she might not listen to reason, "allow Comstock to go, my dear. He is a powerful fellow, and I am persuaded he will travel more swiftly, and with less chance of falling."

"Yes, of course. I was not thinking. You will travel faster than me. There can be no doubt of it."

She looked up at the man, and when she attempted to thank him he silenced her with a wave of his hand. "No need for that, miss."

Nodding, she said, "Go then, please. And hurry."

The instant Comstock turned and sped away, Isobel got back down on her knees and crawled to the cliff edge. "Robert?" she called.

"I am here," he replied, his voice sounding even fainter than it had moments before.

A cold shaft of fear shot through Isobel, and she wondered if Robert's injuries were more severe than he had admitted.

"Do not lose hope," she called to him, "for we have thought of a plan to rescue you."

"I am happy to hear it," he said, "for at the moment I seem excessively dull-witted, and can think of nothing constructive." After a silence that lasted several seconds, he called up to her, "What is your plan? Never tell me you have learned to fly, after all."

"No," she replied, "I . . . I still have not that ability." His show of humor was nearly Isobel's undoing, and she was obliged to swallow hard to keep at bay the sobs that threatened to overcome her. Not wanting Robert to know how frightened she was for him, she tried to keep her voice steady. "Because none of us can fly, we had to come up with an alternate plan."

"We?"

"The three of us. Mr. Comstock, Mr. Wolcott, and me. At the moment, Mr. Comstock is hurrying to the meadow where we left the phaeton, his objective to fetch a rope so we can pull you up. He should return within a short time."

"Excellent," Robert said. "I shall be here."

"See that you are."

Isobel had said Comstock would return shortly, but the time seemed to drag at a snail's pace, with every second like a minute and every minute an hour. Finally, when at least half an hour had passed, and she thought she must surely scream from the agony of waiting, helpless to do anything but call down words of encouragement to Robert, she heard Comstock's heavy footfalls. "Thank you," she whispered, her words a prayer.

"He has returned," she yelled to Robert.

She received no reply, but at that moment she was too elated to notice and so very grateful to their rescuer, who had just came into view. Somewhere along the way Comstock had lost his beaver hat, and though his brown hair was blown every which way by the wind and beads of perspiration showed on his forehead and on his upper lip, his breathing was only slightly labored. He must have brought every inch of rope the orange-haired duo owned, for he wore a thick coil of the hemp on either shoulder, like oversize braid on military epaulets.

When he came to stand near the edge, Isobel got to her feet and moved out of his way so as not to hamper his efforts. "Bless you, sir, for your speed and for your help."

"Mr. Montford," he called, "this is Jethro Comstock talking, and I 'ave got two stout ropes with me. 'Ere is my plan, but if you've a better notion, you've but to say so. I'll take no offense. Otherwise, I will lower the first rope until you tell me to stop. When there is sufficient for you to tie around your waist, just give an 'oller, and I'll desist. Once you 'ave the first rope tied securely I'll anchor it, then lower the second rope and pull you up."

He waited for several seconds, and when there was no reply, he called again. "Mr. Montford?"

Still no response.

Isobel drew close again. "Robert? Answer me, Robert."

Comstock bent quickly, then stretched out on his stomach once again where he could look over the side of the ledge. For a large man, he was surprisingly agile. "Tarnation," he muttered.

Isobel had been holding her breath, but now she let it out in one quick *whoosh.* "What is it? What has happened to Robert? What did you see?"

" 'E isn't moving, miss, and it's my guess 'e 'as lost consciousness."

"Lost—" Her voice almost failed her as she realized all the perils that threatened the man she loved. "What if he should move? You said the ledge was small. What if when he regains consciousness, he rolls forward and . . . ?" She could not finish the question, for to hear the answer would be like cutting her heart from her chest.

Willing herself to remain calm, she asked a more productive question. "What can we do? Have you an alternate plan?"

"Mayhap."

Comstock looked around him, as if searching for something. He muttered a blasphemous oath, then added, "Where's a bleedin' tree when a body needs one?"

Isobel ignored both the oath and the swearing. "You *do* have something in mind. Tell me, sir. Perhaps I can help."

"Beggin' your pardon, miss, but it's a tree I'm needing. One strong enough to 'old me, so I can tie the rope around me and climb down for Mr. Montford."

When Cecil Wolcott spoke, the sound surprised Isobel, for she had forgotten the man was there. "Perhaps I could hold the rope, Comstock, while you—"

"I'm eighteen stone if I'm an ounce, sir. Like as not, we'd both 'ave a speedy trip to the muck below."

No one spoke for a full minute, each lost in thought. Then Isobel was struck with an idea. "What about me, Mr. Comstock? You could tie the rope around me, then lower me to Robert, where I could then secure—"

"No!" Cecil Wolcott stepped forward, as if he meant to stop her by brute force if necessary. "You cannot do it. I forbid you to risk your life."

Isobel had no time to wonder why a man who held her in abhorrence should consider he had a right to forbid her anything. Instead, she focused her attention on Comstock. "I weigh no more than eight stone. A man of your strength should have no trouble bearing my weight."

"No trouble at all, miss, but—"

"There are no *buts*. It is our only option if we are to save Robert. And," she added, a catch in her throat, "we *must* save him."

Comstock reached to his shoulder and removed the first rope. "We'll tie it around your middle first, miss, then loop it around each . . . er . . . upper limb. That will relieve some of the strain on your ribs."

"Do it, sir. And never mind the niceties. I promise you I am not missish."

Taking her at her word, Comstock acted quickly. First he wound the rope around her middle and made a slip knot. Then he passed the length between her ankles and pulled it up so he could loop it around first her right thigh, then her left. He finished by slipping the remaining rope back through the knot and pulling it taut.

Isobel's skirt was pulled up, revealing a scandalous amount of shin and knee, but she did not hesitate long enough to suffer from embarrassment. Instead, she went directly to the edge of the cliff. "Now, sir, do I climb down, or—"

"Let me do all the work."

Having said this, he wrapped the middle of the rope around his left forearm then passed it over his left shoulder, across his back, and around to the right of his ribs. He had tied a handkerchief around his right hand, to offer some protection while the rope was fed across his palm. "I'll let you down easy as I can, miss, but you keep your hands and feet free should you need to protect yourself from crashing against the rock wall."

"Isobel," Wolcott said, "I beg of you, reconsider. Wait until I can fetch help. Or let me go in your stead. I cannot bear to think of you doing anything so dangerous. Please, my dear."

His plea sounded so genuine that Isobel spared a moment to look at him. He was frightened for her; she could see the fear in his eyes. Why he should suddenly be concerned she could not even imagine, but for the moment she had more important considerations. "I am ready, Mr. Comstock."

"Go when you will, miss."

After taking a deep breath, Isobel backed over the edge, giving her weight and her life into a stranger's keeping. The sudden shock of the drop made her gasp, and the pressure of the ropes against her ribs and thighs was more painful than she could have imagined. Still, she welcomed the pain, for it kept her from thinking of the chasm below. If she let herself dwell upon the possibility of falling, she would be unable to move. For that reason, she gave all her energy to thinking of Robert, and what she must do when she reached him.

Her descent went swiftly, and before she had time to realize how far she had come, the toes of her boots touched something solid.

"She has reached the ledge," she heard someone yell. Daring to look up, she saw Cecil Wolcott's face. He was lying on his stomach, leaning over to watch so he could tell Comstock what was happening.

"Easy. Easy," Wolcott shouted. "An inch more. Another. Easy does it."

Another second and her feet touched down solidly.

"Belay!" Wolcott shouted, and immediately the steady feeding of the rope ceased.

Following Comstock's instructions, Isobel placed her hands against the chalk face. It was damp from the spray of the waterfall, but to a woman who had just been hanging in midair it felt comfortingly solid. Aware that the feeling of solidity was an illusion, she warned herself not to become careless.

Reminding herself not to look down, she eased her feet forward until they touched something. That *something* moaned, and Isobel's heart began to race with happiness. Robert was alive. Exercising caution, she knelt slowly, then moved her hands to a warmer, and infinitely dearer, face.

"Robert," she whispered.

When he did not respond, she did as she had been instructed and gave the rope two tugs. Immediately, the second rope was dropped over the cliff edge. Fortunately, it landed practically on Isobel's head, so she was not obliged to move any to reach it. Unfortunately, getting it around Robert's waist proved more difficult than she had imagined, and it might have been impossible if he had not regained consciousness for a moment.

"Isobel," he said, blinking his eyes, "my sweet Isobel. Are you a dream?"

"No," she said, "I am real. I came down to get you, and if you will sit up just a little and let me fasten this rope around you, I will show you how to fly."

Fifteen

Once the rope was securely tied around Robert's waist Isobel gave her own rope two tugs, the sign she and Comstock had agreed upon to mean that she was ready to be pulled back up. Almost before she finished the second tug, she felt herself being lifted from the narrow ledge. "Watch me fly," she called to Robert, "for in a very short time it will be your turn."

Her ascent was swift and bumpy, and several times she was obliged to use her feet to keep herself from being smashed against the side of the mountain. Still, she made it up and over the edge without any real mishap.

"Praise be," Cecil Wolcott said as he grabbed at Isobel's outstretched hands and pulled her the final few inches, then helped her to her feet. She was still attempting to stand on decidedly rubbery legs when, to her surprise, Wolcott threw his arms around her and embraced her. "My dear girl," he said, his voice choked with emotion, "you are safe."

"Sir," she said, extricating herself from his hold, "I thank you for your concern, but there is no time to lose. Robert must be brought up as soon as possible, and I must see if Mr. Comstock needs any help."

"Of course," Wolcott said, stepping back, "forgive me. I was overcome with gratitude at your safe return."

With no time to ponder that very odd, unexpected remark, Isobel hurried over to Comstock to offer her assistance. Cecil Wolcott was but a few seconds behind her, offering his services, as well. Comstock was acknowledged to be the person in charge, and he instructed Wolcott to take up the end of the rope and stand behind him. "If you please, miss, you can 'elp best by keeping me advised on 'ow the ascent is progressing. Look over the edge, as your fa—that is, Mr. Wolcott 'ere—did when you were dangling precarious like, and instruct me when to pull."

Without hesitation, Isobel did the man's bidding, lying on her stomach and leaning her head over until she could see the ledge. "Robert?"

"I am here," he replied, his voice sounding a little stronger than it had earlier.

"Are you ready to fly?"

"Ready," he replied.

Isobel looked back at Comstock, who nodded; then she shouted, "Now!"

She heard a grunt; then the rope that was quite near her shoulder became taut and began to inch its way slowly past her.

"I see him," she yelled.

When she spared a moment to look behind her at the two men doing the pulling, she wished she had not done so, for their teeth were clamped shut and their faces were already red with the exertion of hoisting a man of fully twelve stone. She had never doubted that Comstock could manage her weight, but now she realized just how much strength was required to lift a man of Robert's muscular physique.

When the veins in Comstock's neck became engorged, and his left arm began to quiver, fear made Isobel turn back quickly to find Robert, to see how much farther he had to come. His ascent was not as swift as hers had been, and he hung suspended in space, a good ten feet below them. Thankfully, he was conscious, and held the rope with one hand while using the other to protect himself against the sharp sides of the mountain.

"Another ten feet," she yelled to Comstock. Then, to encourage Robert, she said, "You are halfway here. Just another minute or so, and all will be well." Isobel prayed she spoke the truth, for how could she live in a world without Robert?

To her great relief, she was not obliged to discover how a woman survived the loss of the only man she had ever loved, for her prayers were answered. While the men behind her groaned in apparent distress, Isobel saw Robert's uplifted hand. It was within reach, and she grabbed it, clutching it with all her might as if she, and not Robert, were in need of rescue.

"I have his hand," she yelled over her shoulder, and while the tears coursed down her cheeks she scurried backward to make room for Robert. Disregarding the unladylike picture she must make— crawling like a snake on its belly, with her thighs still bound by the rope and her skirt up, exposing her legs—Isobel remained on the ground, waiting, her heart beating so hard it felt like a giant drum inside her chest.

She did not draw breath between the time she saw the top of Robert's head and the moment he lay beside her on the chalky ledge. Judging by the labored, rasping sound of Robert's inhalations, he had been equally breathless. Now, however, they both took deep, reviving gulps of air, neither speaking, merely locking their fingers together as if vowing never to let go.

As for Comstock and Cecil Wolcott, they fell to the ground as soon as Robert was safe, and that was where they still lay when a pair of climbers came running up the path, followed by one of the orange-haired men. "My word," the first climber said, dropping his coil of rope and looking around him at the four exhausted people. "Which one of you needs help first?

"It is difficult to tell," said his companion.

It was Isobel who finally answered the young man's question. "We are all of us well, sir. Wonderfully, gloriously well."

The climbers assisted them by making a pack saddle of their crossed arms and carrying Robert back down to his phaeton. Theirs was not an easy journey, and when they reached the carriage Isobel was dismayed to discover that she was not to be allowed to accompany Robert back to Montford House.

"It's for the best, miss," Comstock said, climbing up beside Robert. Taking the reins and clicking his tongue, he set the team in motion. It was left to Cecil Wolcott to give Isobel a place in his carriage.

At her insistence, the gentleman kept the phaeton

in sight at all times. Once, when they were still a good two miles from the estate, Cecil Wolcott said he had something important he wished to discuss with Isobel. "At least *I* believe it is important. What you may think remains to be seen."

Isobel's concern for Robert filled her thoughts, and she had little interest in anything else. "You were most helpful at Cromer Ridge, Mr. Wolcott, and for that I thank you very much, but no matter what it is that concerns you, it must wait upon Robert's return to health."

His handsome face betrayed his annoyance, but he did not pursue the matter. "Whatever you say, my dear."

It was not to be wondered at that Agatha Montford and her friend, Lady Baysworth, gasped when they saw Robert being assisted into the house. "My boy!" his mother said, her pretty, hazel eyes wide with concern. "Are you all right?"

Robert assured her that his injury was probably nothing more than a bruised rib—"Not a thing for you to be worried about," he said—but the lady would not give over her motherly concern.

Calling to Kendrick to send a groom for the apothecary on the instant, she preceded her son and a rather disheveled-looking Jethro Comstock up the stairs. Then, to Isobel's surprise, Agatha Montford paused and leaned over the stair rail. "Cecil," she said, "please come with me, for I need your support."

Wolcott complied without hesitation, and when Isobel took a step toward the stairs, as if she meant to follow behind them, Lady Baysworth caught her arm and held her back. "Stay," she said. "Let his mother see to him for the moment."

"But—"

"Robert told us his injury was not serious, and I, for one, am inclined to believe him. He is, after all, a sensible fellow. Besides, I should like to know what happened. When a young woman comes home from what should have been an unexceptional morning's excursion and her clothes are crumpled and filthy, and her hair is falling all about her shoulders, my curiosity becomes so intense it is not to be borne."

Isobel's hand went instinctively to her hair. As her ladyship had said, it was a shambles. Seeing no way to escape explanation, she told the entire story—beginning with the pleasure she and Robert experienced as they attempted to uncover the bones of the dinosaur, continuing through to the accident that took the life of Willem Potter and very nearly claimed Robert as well.

Edith Baysworth listened with avid interest, holding all comment until Isobel had completed her story. "And you truly went down to rescue dear Robert? You allowed yourself to be dropped over the side of the cliff into nothing but thin air?"

Though it sounded quite harebrained the way her ladyship related it, Isobel could not deny her part, so she nodded.

Lady Baysworth sighed. "What an adventure. I was always a rather shy young woman, never brave, but what you did today is just the kind of thing Fiona would have done. You are so like her, my love."

Their conversation was interrupted by Cecil Wolcott, who came to tell them that Robert was sitting up in his bed and had declared himself famished.

"When he called for food, I knew he was out of danger, so—"

"So you came," Lady Baysworth said, "to finish that thing you had meant to do earlier . . . have your talk with our dear Isobel."

"As you say, my friend—nay, my sister-in-law—it is time and more that I told Isobel why I followed her to Cromer Ridge."

Earlier, Isobel had been too busy to question Wolcott's sudden appearance at the ridge, but now she looked at him, her fixed stare asking the question for her.

Her question was unspoken, and so was his answer. He simply withdrew something from inside his coat and offered the small object to her. It was a cream-colored ribbon, the one she had worn around her throat the evening before, and her mother's brooch was still pinned to the velvet. "My brooch," she said, hugging the jewelry to her heart. "I looked all over for it last night. I wondered where I could have dropped it."

"In the book room," Wolcott said. "I picked it up just after you left."

Isobel studied the dual masks of comedy and tragedy. "This belonged to my mother."

"It belonged to Fiona," he said.

At his absurd words, Isobel's head snapped up, and she glared at the man. "How *dare* you say that? This belonged to my mother. It was given to her by my father, before I was born."

"I know," he said, his voice little more than a whisper. "I gave it to her for her eighteenth birthday."

"You lie! Oh, not about her eighteenth birthday, for my father told me the story often, but everything else you say is untrue. My father had this brooch made for—"

"For my wife, Fiona."

When Isobel refused to listen, Wolcott bid her close her eyes and run her finger around the thin filigree that joined the two masks. "There, skillfully hidden, are two initials. You will find that one of them is an F, for Fiona. The other is a C, for Cecil." He cleared his throat, almost as if the youthful sentiment still had the power to move him. "It was not very original, I know, but at the time I thought it quite romantic."

Isobel felt tears of anger sting at the back of her eyes. Why was he saying these things? Did he dislike her so much? "My father is—was—Thomas Townsend," she said," and he—"

"No," Cecil Wolcott said. "Thomas Townsend was a kind, gentle man, and I am persuaded that he told you what he did thinking it was for the best. But he was a friend to your mother, nothing more. Fiona was my wife, and *I* am your father."

Sixteen

Isobel sat quietly upon the grassy sward, her feet tucked beneath the skirt of her yellow dress, and watched the dozen or so ducks that floated placidly on the gray-blue waters of the pond. The shallow pond was in the center of the green at Ashbridge, Kent, and though it was only mid-August the tips of the pear tree leaves were already beginning to show signs of color, reminding one and all that autumn was but a few weeks away.

From Isobel's calm exterior, a passerby might have been forgiven for thinking the young lady had not a care in the world. He would have been wrong. She had returned to Kent because she needed to be near the home she had known with Thomas Townsend, the man she had always believed was her father. She needed to recall their time together.

The thatched-roof cottage where she and her father had lived was now occupied by a family Isobel had never met before, but when she explained to the young woman with the baby upon her hip exactly who she was the woman invited her to come inside. After a short visit in which Isobel was served strong, pungent tea and freshly-baked bread at the kitchen table, the woman graciously allowed her guest to wander through their home, both upstairs and down, giving her some privacy while she touched walls, doors, and windows that evoked recollections of her childhood.

After her traverse down memory lane, Isobel had sought the familiarity of the pond rather than return to the little inn where she had procured a room—at least, the pond was as she remembered it. The ducks still quacked at one another and at every falling leaf, and they still rushed to the water's edge each time someone approached, apparently hoping the newcomer had brought chunks of bread to toss onto the water.

How strange it was to view something so familiar yet feel so unconnected with it all. This was Isobel's home, and yet it was not. People passed her on the high street, people she had never seen before, and they looked at her as if she were a stranger, a visitor to their village, someone who did not belong.

Perhaps they were right.

Isobel had thought she belonged in Ashbridge. Of course, she had also thought she belonged to Thomas Townsend, and he to her. Now she knew that was not true. All her life she had believed she was Thomas Townsend's daughter, and in all the ways that truly mattered to a child, he had been her father. He had cared for her, fed her, clothed her, bound up her childhood wounds—both physical and emotional—and lavished upon her the abundance of love that was in his heart.

Could a child ask for more? Was the truth so very important?

Though her head answered, "Yes," her heart said, "No."

Isobel had experienced a wonderful childhood, and that happy time was given to her by a man whom she adored, a man who loved her in return. It was that man who had taught her to tell the truth. Always. Now she had discovered that the stories he had told her were a fabrication, that he had deceived her from the very beginning of her life.

And yet, how could she censure Thomas Townsend for his actions? True, he was a gentleman of deception, but did that deceit make him any less praiseworthy for the life he had given her?

Isobel answered that question with a decided shake of her head. She knew the man, and she knew in her heart that he had done what he thought was best. He had deceived her, but the deception was meant to give her a feeling of stability, assurance, continuity.

Thomas Townsend was her father in all the best sense of the word. He could have washed his hands of her, sent her to an orphanage, and no one would have taken him to task. Instead, he gave a motherless infant his name, his home, and his love. And Isobel loved him for it. She always would.

Just as she would always love Robert Montford.

At the thought of Robert, Isobel had to swallow a sob. She missed him so much. More than she had ever imagined. She had been reasonably content with her life before she met him, but now, after getting to know him and growing to love him, her life seemed empty, pointless, and the loneliness was like a constant pain in her heart. The pain throbbed from the moment she awoke each morning to the moment she cried herself to sleep each night.

She had not seen Robert, or anyone else from Montford House, since the twenty-third of July. Three weeks, two days, and seven hours ago she had boarded the mailcoach for London, leaving Norfolk and everyone in it behind.

"At the very least," Agatha Montford had said, "wait until Robert returns from the coroner's inquest regarding Willem Potter's demise. I am persuaded my son did not know that you meant to leave this morning."

"He knew," Isobel replied.

Of course he knew. It was not as though she had not planned to leave; she had told them all from the moment she entered the house that she would leave within two weeks. They all knew she had signed a contract with The Haymarket Theater. Still, the women had pled with her not to go, and Lady Baysworth had cried copious tears.

"Please stay," her ladyship had begged. "Better still, accompany me to my home. Make it your home. I mean to leave Montford House in a matter of days, so that I will be at Bay Manor when my son arrives. We can wait for him together. Your cousin will be so happy to make your acquaintance."

Isobel had kissed the lady's cheek, but she had remained adamant about leaving.

As for Cecil Wolcott, he said nothing. He merely looked at her. In his eyes was such regret that Isobel very nearly agreed to stay. But she did not. She did let Wolcott's man, Mr. Zell, drive her to Gresham, and even accepted the letter the valet pressed into her hand just before the coachman cracked the whip over the horses' heads.

The letter was from Cecil Wolcott.

> *My Dear Daughter,*
>
> *I understand why you feel you must leave, for you have much to sort through and settle in your mind. I have only two things I wish to say to you, and they are: If and when you come to terms with who you are and what part of your life you will allow me to share, please come to me. Wolcott Park will always be your home. I want to get to know you, and I want you to get to know me and your uncle. I love and admire you already, and perhaps one day you will come to like me, as well.*
>
> *Secondly, I beg you not to throw away a possible life with Robert Montford. The young man loves you, I can see it in his eyes. And I believe you love him, as well. Do not follow the foolish path taken by me and your mother. Whatever your reasons, and I am sure you consider them valid, do not give up this chance for happiness.*
>
> *Whatever you decide, and wherever you go, know always that you are in my thoughts.*
>
> *Your father*

Isobel had read the letter many times in the past three weeks, and with each reading she felt she knew Cecil Wolcott a little better. She had let go of her animosity toward him, for she truly believed that he would have found Fiona if he could, and that he would have made a home for Fiona, and for her. Still, she needed time to learn to think of him as her real father.

Time, the poets said, healed all things. Isobel doubted it, for even if she lived to be one hundred she would never forget Robert, never forget the man she loved with all her heart. Nor could time ever dim the recollection of her inexpressible joy at seeing him being pulled up and over the edge of the cliff at Cromer Ridge.

There were not enough years in one lifetime to erase the memory of Robert's strong arms wrapped around her, or the feel of his warm lips pressed against hers. And how could she ever forget his slow smile? Or the way his brown eyes . . .

Her thoughts were interrupted by the sudden frenzied quacking of the ducks, who turned as one and swam to the other side of the pond. When Isobel looked behind her to discover who had provoked such a frenzy in the fowl, she could not believe her eyes. It was as if by thinking of Robert she had conjured him up, for he stood not ten feet away from her. Tall. Handsome. And furious. So angry that it was all she could do not to emulate the ducks and run away.

"So," he said, not bothering with a greeting, "I find you at last."

Isobel jumped to her feet. "Robert. What are you doing here?"

"More to the point," he said, his face set in a scowl, "what are *you* doing here? You were supposed to be in London, at The Haymarket Theater. Have you any idea how I felt when I discovered that you had written to the manager asking to be released from your contract?"

"Why, no. I—"

"The manager let me read your letter, but it gave no address where you could be contacted. I was frantic, for I had no idea how or where to find you. My godmother constantly remarks the similarity between you and her sister, but I never expected you to follow in Fiona's footsteps."

Isobel thought for a moment that he referred to Fiona's elopement, but then she realized he meant that like her mother she had left London and come to Ashbridge. "The difference," she said, "is that my mother came to Kent *with* Thomas Townsend. I came here to find him."

With her words, the anger that had filled Robert moments ago seemed to leave him. Now, all he felt was relief that Isobel was safe. "And did you find him?" he asked.

She nodded. "I never really lost him. You cannot lose someone who owns a portion of your heart."

"Tell that to Cecil Wolcott! I daresay he would not agree."

He regretted the words as soon as they left his mouth, but she did not flinch at the rebuke. Instead, she continued to stare at him, her chin up and her head high. Always so honest, even with herself.

As he looked at her, all Robert could think about was how dauntless she was, never giving in when life— or people—treated her unfairly. Isobel Townsend had courage enough for ten people. What other woman would have let herself be lowered down the mountain to save him? He knew of no other. "I never thanked you," he said, "for teaching me to fly."

She smiled then, and it was as if his weeks of searching had been rewarded. "You are welcome, sir."

"Am I?"

Something in his tone made Isobel's heart begin to race. "I do not know what you mean."

"You said I was welcome. I merely wished to know how much. A little bit welcome? Very welcome?"

When she did not reply, he said, "Are you the least bit happy to see me?"

Happy? If he only knew.

He had stopped several feet from her, and now he stepped closer, close enough to take her hand in his. "You must answer me," he said. "I know you will speak truthfully, so tell me now if you wish I had not come to find you. Shall I go away? Shall I take with me all the love I have in my heart? The love I have for you alone?"

Isobel's lungs seemed to have failed her, for she had difficulty drawing breath enough to say the words. "You love me?"

"Of course I do."

He caught her other hand and began to pull her ever so gently toward him, not stopping until she was so close she could smell the delicious spicy aroma that clung to his skin. "I thought you knew," he said. "When I kissed you, and you kissed me back with such honesty, such unreserved response, I thought you knew how much I loved you."

She shook her head. "I knew only that I loved you. With all my heart."

That seemed to be all the answer Robert needed, for he caught her in his arms and pulled her close against his chest. Then slowly, agonizingly slowly, he lowered his head and covered her lips with his own.

The kiss was magic. It sent her soaring to the heavens, while at the same time it bound her forever to the man she adored. It was only when she heard the quacking of the ducks that Isobel remembered that she and Robert were in a public place. Regretfully, she placed her hands against Robert's chest and pushed ever so slightly. He ended the kiss, but he did not release her.

"Robert," she said, looking to her left and then to her right, to assure herself that they had not been observed, "you must not kiss me here, for we are standing in the middle of the village green. Anyone might be watching."

"True," he said, gazing down at her with that teasing light in his eyes. "Naturally, you would not wish to ruin the reputation you had here as a child. 'Sugar and spice,' I believe you said."

"Exactly."

He bent and nibbled softly at a spot just beneath her ear, sending waves of heat through Isobel's body. Then, when her knees had grown so weak they refused to bear her weight and she was obliged to lean against Robert for support, he found a twin of that spot beneath her other ear.

As if his purpose in life was to torment her, he touched the tip of his tongue to her skin, and when she moaned he trailed little kisses up her neck and across her chin. He stopped just at the corner of her mouth.

"Do not stop," she begged, turning her mouth up to receive his kiss.

"But, my love," he said. His tone one of mock surprise. "What of your reputation? What of your little girl image of sugar and spice?"

For her answer, Isobel slipped her hands up his muscular arms and over his shoulders, then locked her fingers behind his neck. "I never liked sugar," she said, giving a tug that brought his face back down to hers.

"My thoughts exactly," he said. Then he claimed her lips once again.

Epilogue

"The post has finally arrived," Isobel said, ducking automatically so that her forehead did not collide with the low lintel of the sheepherder's hut. "There is a letter from your mother. From Mrs. Wolcott, I should say. She writes to inform us that she and my father have returned from their wedding trip, and that your tenants find their new landlord a knowledgeable and admirable fellow."

"I am not at all surprised," Robert said. "I would not have left the estate in his hands had I not had faith in his ability to run it properly."

Isobel shuffled through the stack of letters, pausing to look at the date on one sent to her by her cousin, Gordon Baysworth. "This letter is more than three months old! I wager it has been sitting in the post office in Istanbul for weeks."

Robert put aside the bone fragments he had been cataloging in his journal and pushed his chair away from the worktable. "It is my opinion, my love, that the Turks who are entrusted with delivering the post do not consider us high on their list of important stops. After all, what can an English couple who are foolish enough to spend the winter in a hut on the side of a mountain want with letters?"

Isobel laughed. "You may be right about that. Though I did not understand even half of what was said between the two men who made the delivery, I believe the word 'foolish' might have been in there somewhere." She tossed the letters onto a bed that took up a third of the room, then removed her thick, fleece-lined coat.

"You should have seen the men," she said. "I believe they were twins, for they rode identical donkeys, and they both wore enormous turbans and sported mustaches that were waxed so stiff they resembled horns."

"Do you refer to the men, my love, or to the donkeys?"

"Robert! Must you tease me about everything?"

"Yes," he replied, "I believe I must."

She laughed again, and her husband caught her hand and pulled her down onto his lap. When she landed against him, he placed a quick kiss upon her lips. "That," he said, "is your reward for being such a good sport about my teasing."

"Pooh," Isobel said. "Is that all I get, one little quick kiss? I am a much better sport than that."

It was Robert's time to laugh. "How much better?"

"Here," she said, winding her arms around his neck, "let me show you."

ABOUT THE AUTHOR

Martha Kirkland lives with her family in Georgia. She is the author of five Zebra Regency romances, and has written many Regency romances for Signet. Martha loves to hear from her readers, and you may write to her c/o Zebra Books. Please include a self-addressed stamped envelope if you wish a response.

<u>BOOK YOUR PLACE ON OUR WEBSITE</u>
AND MAKE THE
<u>READING CONNECTION!</u>

We've created a customized website just for our very special readers, where you can get the inside scoop on everything that's going on with Zebra, Pinnacle and Kensington books.

When you come online, you'll have the exciting opportunity to:

- View covers of upcoming books
- Read sample chapters
- Learn about our future publishing schedule (listed by publication month *and author*)
- Find out when your favorite authors will be visiting a city near you
- Search for and order backlist books from our online catalog
- Check out author bios and background information
- Send e-mail to your favorite authors
- Meet the Kensington staff online
- Join us in weekly chats with authors, readers and other guests
- Get writing guidelines
- AND MUCH MORE!

Visit our website at
http://www.zebrabooks.com

LOOK FOR THESE REGENCY ROMANCES